#LucysLetter

The Children of
the Greenhouse Age

A NOVEL

Vincent
Lowry

Book cover design and layout by Ellie Bockert Augsburger
of Creative Digital Studios.
www.CreativeDigitalStudios.com

Cover design features:

Little Girl on a Swing: © Ivan Kopylov / Dollar Photo Club
Red Fire Icon Set: © Seamartini Graphics / Dollar Photo Club
Tree Silhouettes: © lecostaloca / Dollar Photo Club

Editing Services provided by Carl Augsburger of Creative Digital Studios.
www.CreativeDigitalStudios.com

ISBN: 978-0-578-17407-5

For you and your family,
regardless of race or religion,
age or gender,
sexuality or nationality.

Frère Jacques, frère Jacques,
Dormez-vous? Dormez-vous?
Sonnez les matines! Sonnez les matines!
Ding dang dong, ding dang dong.
-Frère Jacques

PART I
FIRE

CHAPTER 1

Lucy Gold only knew two credible facts about her mother: her name was Susan, and she had been in shackles on the day she had given birth to her only child. Everything else about Susan Gold was shrouded in myth and conjecture. If Lucy listened to the incessant teasing of the kids at Richards Middle School, she could count at least a dozen crimes her mother had committed—assault, robbery, and murder, to name just a few. One perfidious boy, Jack Gleeson of the seventh grade, went so far as to claim that Susan had executed three bank tellers at point-blank range, and his dad now owned the gun she had used. Lucy, never shy, pressed Jack to show his evidence.

"You're lying and you know it, Jack!" Lucy said, her voice almost as commanding as that of Clara Gold, her sagacious grandma. "My mother didn't rob a bank or shoot anybody!"

"How do you know?" Jack asked, grinning with three of his playground buddies. Jack's milky white belly always protruded from shirts that were too small for his portly frame. He looked out of place next to his slender friends. "It's true. My dad's a cop. I'll bring the gun in tomorrow!"

Lucy's hazel eyes burned with anger. Her fists were clenched so tightly that her knuckles turned bone white. "You do that, Jack! I bet you all the pearls in the world you don't have it. All the diamonds, too!"

"You'll see, Lucy. Tomorrow I'm going to be rich. I'll get it in the morning from my dad's room and bring it. Meet me at the front gate before school starts."

Lucy said she would, and did. The next day, Jack, and his belly, never showed.

Months later, when Lucy told her grandma about yet another argument she had at school with a different kid in her classroom (a girl, this time), she was promptly told to ignore the gossip and fuss regarding her mother. "Past is past, Lucy-Lu," Grandma Clara said, hunched over the kitchen sink and filling Lucy's cup with a third of her daily ration of water. The digital meter on government-issued "smart-pour" faucet read 4.76. *Past is past* is what Lucy's grandma always said when it came to the subject of her daughter. Nothing more could be discussed after those words were uttered; breaching that invisible wall was as futile as trying to jump to the moon.

"Peanut butter again..." Lucy whined, staring at the lunch her grandma had prepared. The sandwich lay like a flat white brick in the center of potato chips and baby carrots.

Grandma Clara nodded, fixing the bun that held her grey strands of hair in a packed ball. "The market was out of fish, sweetie. Sorry, but this will have to do until I go back again."

Lucy took her water and lunch and made for the backyard patio, her long brunette hair bouncing on her tan shoulders. It was late November, but the air felt like it always did to Lucy this time of year: hot and soupy with no chance of relief. It was as if she were under the sheets of her bed, playing games with her cat, and unable to toss those sheets aside when her lungs screamed for help. Those sheets were ever-present over Lake Sabrina, relentlessly baking the land.

"Timmy givin' you problems again?"

Lucy, sitting on the doorstep, moved her eyes from the few bites she had taken from her sandwich and fixed them on Uncle Neil. He rocked in a wicker swing while clad in jeans and a grey t-shirt, an unopened beer in hand. The old swing creaked as it slowly swayed back and forth, a forlorn sound that seemed to be the voice of the aged two-story house itself that Lucy, Uncle Neil, and Grandma Clara called home.

"It's nothing," Lucy said, depositing a carrot in her mouth while shifting weight from her right side to her left. The doorstep was in the shade, but it was still hot as hell—stinging her just sitting on it.

Uncle Neil's weathered, leathery face studied Lucy as he effortlessly cracked open his beer can without looking down. Imported alcohol was one of the few items not rationed or regulated by the Drought Relief Act. Compromises had to be made; Uncle Neil liked to joke to his card buddies that there was a lobbyist guardian angel looking over his shoulder, keeping an eye out on his only luxury.

"If that Timmy fella keeps jawing, I'm going to fix that mouth with my fist," Uncle Neil said, training his blue eyes on an emaciated crow scavenging for food.

"It's not Timmy."

"No? I thought you said Rachel left to live with her cousins? Flew the coop, like everyone else in this damn state."

"It's not Rachel, either. I don't want to talk about it, Uncle Neil. Okay?"

Lucy took another bite of her sandwich, then washed it down with water that had a hint of a taste of lemon. Lucy hated the artificial flavor. She knew they just put it in to mask the chemical byproduct of the pipes and containers in which the water had been filtered and pumped.

"Suit yourself," Uncle Neil replied, sipping from his beer, letting out a fart as he did so. Lucy used to laugh whenever he, or anyone else, passed gas. But that was a different Lucy of many rusty sunsets ago, a little girl who didn't have to come to terms with her family's past.

The gaunt crow took flight, either frightened by the sound of the flatulence or disappointed by the prospects of food.

"Ever talk to that Rachel friend of yours, by the way?" Uncle Neil finally asked after a long pause. "Was it New Hampshire she moved to?"

"Maine," Lucy said, shooing a fly from her plate, then wiping a patch of sweat from her forehead. The temperature gauge behind her read 108°F. Uncle Neil had nailed it up on a support beam two summers back, the day Lake Sabrina hit its second hottest afternoon on record: 129°F. "Near Augusta, they said."

"That's right," her uncle replied, kicking his swing out and nodding as if the location had been told to him one minute ago rather than four months. "I remember all the hype they spit at us now. The vineyards from heaven. The shorts and shirts you could wear year-round. The beaches of paradise."

"Yeah, well, I don't look for her on the sites anymore, and she only called me once. A year ago."

"For your 11th birthday," Grandma Clara said from inside the house, standing just a few feet behind Lucy. She wore a faded apron that said *To Cook is to Love,* an anniversary gift from her late husband. He had also given her a matching chef's hat, but that had been lost long ago. "Such a sweet girl. Too bad they left."

"Good riddance," Uncle Neil shot back. "They were snotty and never did anything worth a rat's turd around here anyway. Too bad they didn't go southeast and wash away with everyone else."

"Hush," Grandma Clara said sternly. "Watch that language around Lucy, Joe."

Joe was Neil's middle name. It often took priority over his first whenever he took his opinions too far, which happened frequently when he drank, lobbyist guardian angel or not.

"I've heard turd a million times, Grandma," Lucy said, giggling as she said it.

"Well I don't like that word. It's uncivilized."

"Uncivilized!" Now it was Uncle Neil who was laughing. His laughter soon dissolved into a raspy cough, which lasted for a minute before he could speak again. "Hell...take a look at our American Dream, Mom. Our plot of the great frontier."

"Hell, too. That's another word not to be used around this house. And our property is just fine. Got it better than most folks."

Lucy stared at the last remaining bites of her sandwich, swearing to herself that she heard this conversation between her uncle and grandma at least two or three times a week...perhaps more. She had become inured to it. It was always about who had stayed, moved, gone broke, gone six feet under, and gotten into trouble. That was the catalyst. The conversation then turned to the current state of California, the 86-year-long drought that was punishing all corners of what her uncle called the big three F's: farms, forests, and fields. It was a pointless conversation as far as Lucy was concerned. Even at the age of twelve, she knew the three F's had already burned or withered beyond repair. She could see it around her at Lake Sabrina: black jagged stumps that had once been healthy trees surrounded by layers of ash where the undergrowth had once flourished; abandoned motorboats lying in the sand beside crumbling docks that hadn't seen water in fifteen presidents; faded white marks on tall boulders serving as a reminder of the days when the lake had once been a popular fishing and swimming getaway for residents of Los Angeles, Fresno, San Francisco, and Vegas.

Lucy found it ironic that she knew so much about the history of Lake Sabrina—established in 1907 by the damming of Bishop Creek and named after Mrs. Sabrina Hobbs, wife of the first General Manager of California Nevada Power Company, the company that built the dam—and yet so little about her own history. Grandma Clara's selective conversations, her insistence that *past is past*, and Uncle Neil's typical tangents ensured Lucy's ignorance would remain fixed for quite some time unless she came up with a crafty strategy to change things. Her strategy needed to bypass her Grandma's protectiveness, steer through her uncle's randomness, and do it at a time when only Lucy would be listening so that others wouldn't tease her even more when the truth finally came out.

What? Did you say Susan Gold was a serial killer and a disease-spreading whore who slept with everyone in town? I knew it! Boy, I can't wait to share this with everyone!

Lucy could just picture the kids at school going nuts upon hearing news that was juicer than the gossip they had cooked up over the years. Kids— specifically the pusillanimous ones with shirts too small for their fat-ass piggy bellies—would make every effort to embarrass and demean her so they could get a couple of stupid laughs at her expense. Her mother was just a joke to them. They had dehumanized her as if she were a beast, an animal whose name was spoken only when needed to amplify the punch line of their comic gag.

Lucy swore she would make sure their ignorance would remain all the way to their graves; they could gossip and laugh all they wanted now, but someday a nettlesome part of them (albeit only a fraction of the curiosity that boiled in Lucy's veins) would eat at their core and force them to wonder just what the hell really happened to Susan Gold. They would never know the truth.

Lucy would. She already had a plan in mind.

"You finish those carrots, Lucy-Lu," Grandma Clara said, now outside and brushing off the crumbs on her *To Cook is to Love* apron. "You need real vitamins. Those inhalants don't do a darn thing as far as I've seen."

"They taste kinda yucky, Grandma. Dry."

Grandma Clara's eyes shot to Uncle Neil. If a look could kill, Uncle Neil's body would have burst into flames right at that moment, his remains looking much like the nearby scorched tree stumps.

"What?" Uncle Neil asked innocently.

"I told you to put that bag away yesterday when you got it out. You left it on the counter again, didn't you?"

"Now hold on here…"

"Didn't you?"

Her eyes tore through Uncle Neil. He dropped his gaze, surrendering.

"I cannot believe you, Joe. Now I get to add another item to my list. You know how expensive those veggie bags were the last time I went? Double what they were last year. And they're making 'em smaller, too. I swear in two years it will just be the bag they're selling."

Lucy giggled. She immediately stopped when her grandma's glare burned in her direction.

"Won't happen again, Mom," Uncle Neil said. If it weren't for the beer in his hand, at that moment he could have passed for a repentant, overgrown choirboy. "I promise."

Grandma Clara shook her head, brushed her apron one last time, and reentered the house. When the sound of her footsteps passed a safe distance, Uncle Neil turned to Lucy.

"You little skunk. *They taste kinda yucky...*"

"Sorry, Uncle Neil. I shouldn't have said that. I completely forgot what you told me last night. Thanks for not ratting me out. I'll remember next time."

Uncle Neil just shrugged it off as if he'd been through a million of Grandma Clara's scoldings, which wasn't far from the truth, and raised his beer to his lips. He had his faults: jumping from entry-level job to entry-level job as if playing hopscotch with his career, losing his temper with friends and girlfriends even though they had done little to instigate his verbal outbursts, and spending too much time with his imported liquid luxuries. But no one would ever accuse Neil Gold of not standing by his niece. He was the father she never had, and although he would never win any awards for *Substitute Dad of the Year* with his vices and loose mouth, his net impact on Lucy's life was far more positive and constructive than if he'd never been around.

Part I - Fire

"Uncle Neil…" Lucy said, forcing down the last baby carrot. "Are you playing cards tonight?"

A thin smile creased her uncle's lips. He had a week's worth of stubble on his face, tiny stalks of grey and black. "Ain't it Saturday night, Lucy? Where else would I be if I weren't collecting my paycheck?"

"You think I could come with you?" Lucy asked.

Uncle Neil's head shot back as if he'd been socked in the nose. "Lucy! Tell me you're just playing around? You're not bein' serious, right?"

Lucy's eyes didn't waver. She didn't even blink.

Seeing the determined look in her face seemed to make the colors run out of her uncle's. His typical desert-red complexion became subtly paler, as if he'd just been spared from a car accident.

"No way, Lucy. Ain't gonna happen."

"Why not?"

"Ha! Why not?! Have you lost all the marbles in that little pretty head of yours, Lucy? Do we live in the same house?"

"She won't find out. I promise."

"The hell she won't! Damn woman sleeps like a Doberman pinscher with its ears pricked up. She could hear a mouse on a carpet the next house over. Always been a mystery to me how she ever sleeps at all."

Poker, blackjack, gin rummy—Lucy's uncle could play just about any game involving queens and kings. While he wasn't exactly rolling rich with his earnings, he took home enough to help pay the bills, avoiding Grandma Clara's lectures on his sinful card playing. But taking Lucy with him was another matter.

"I've snuck out on her before. It's not hard."

"Huh? When?"

"With Frank Baker a few times. Last summer." Lucy saw her uncle's eyes bulge; she could guess his next question. "We didn't do anything. Kissed a few times, but that was it. I swear!"

"Grandma would kill you more for that than poker, I'm pretty sure."

"Exactly! All the more reason why doing this isn't so bad. Please Uncle Neil! I really want to go!"

He took the last swig of his beer and stared blankly at the fine print on the side of the can: *Recycle, it's the law*. He knew if they got caught, they'd never hear the end of it from his mother. But he also knew his buddies wouldn't care if Lucy tagged along, so long as the game proceeded without interruptions (such as annoying questions about flushes, straights, and full houses), and as long as she kept her nose out of their personal business. He explained both of these conditions to Lucy. She quickly nodded and smiled, knowing she had won the battle.

"Eleven o'clock we head out," Uncle Neil told Lucy. "Assuming Grandma isn't waiting for us with her fists at the front door."

Lucy jumped up, ran to him, and wrapped her arms around his waist in a strong hug. "Thank you, Uncle Neil! This is so great! I cannot wait!"

"Yes, well..." he said, letting the sentence die, now wishing he hadn't given in so easily. He glanced at the patio door, swearing his mother had heard their every word and was already ready to box their ears.

She wasn't. He could faintly hear her in the kitchen. Lucy drew back from him.

"I'll be ready at 11:00! I promise I won't fall asleep!"

CHAPTER 2

Lucy kept her word. It was the easiest pledge she had ever made in her life, and she could have kept her eyes open for the entire month had she needed to wait that long to carry out her cunning plan, the details of which she had written down in her private journal.

Hiding under her covers with a small book light in her lap, Lucy reread the lines she had just jotted down.

> *11/26 Super excited tonight!!! Finally got the guts to ask, and Uncle agreed! So doubtful at first! Never in a million years did I think it would really happen! A billion! But it is. Bit nervous, though. Okay, I lie...more than a bit. A ton! Grandma will surely murder us if she finds out. Must be ninjas getting out of this dusty old place. 10:46 now! Each minute is soooo long! Like an hour! Come on, clock...*

Her grandma had already checked on her and said sweet dreams before turning out the hallway light at 10:15. Lucy knew there was a good chance she was already asleep now, but it was best to play it safe. She would stay under the covers until her watch—ticking away minute by agonizing minute— reached the agreed-upon time, allowing her to slip out undiscovered.

The fuzzy socks on her feet would dampen the noise of her footsteps on the hardwood floor. They had been a gift from her grandfather. Before he had passed, he gave the socks to Lucy as a birthday present, not knowing he'd picked out a pair that was three times his granddaughter's foot size. Now that they fit, Lucy wore them all the time. They were red, and they matched perfectly with the burgundy blouse she had picked out for the evening, an outfit that also mirrored the color of a pair of heels she had beside her closet, ready for the evening. "They look like a hooker's stilettos," Grandma Clara had said to Lucy three months back upon first seeing them. "You working the streets now, young lady?" Lucy had begged her grandma to let her keep what she had purchased with her own saved money, and she had won the argument because they were her only pair of fancy dress shoes. She'd won a similar victory to keep her first pair of earrings when she had gotten her ears pierced.

Lucy knew full well she'd be overdressed for the group of old fogies downing beers and tossing chips, but she liked it. She felt like an adult. The rules at school and home were unbearably restrictive and dull, and any chance she had to bend those rules to express the feminine vim blossoming within her soul was an opportunity she would not pass up. She needed to show to the world—and even herself—that the door between play dolls and monthly periods had been opened, and that there was no looking back.

"Psst...Lucy? Lucy?"

She removed her bed covers to find her uncle peeking in her bedroom, the door ajar by a few inches. A slice of pale moonlight penetrated the bedroom window and lit the side of Uncle Neil's face, showing a large eye that looked a bit freakish because of its intensity. Had Lucy been sleeping and awakened by such a sight, she would have screamed.

"I'm ready," Lucy replied, sliding off the bed and moving to her shoes as silently as a cat. She retrieved a small backpack from her closet, stuffed the shoes in the largest pocket (wearing them out would have been stupid), and stowed a small black jewelry box in the smallest pocket.

She then glanced at her unmade bed with her journal laying near her pillow. She thought for a second about making some sort of dummy...maybe stuffing the covers to look like a body, or putting a few pillows at such an angle that one might think her head was just hidden because of the way she was sleeping.

"What are you doing?" her uncle whispered. "Come on… Quit messing around."

Lucy turned to her uncle and nodded. Grandma Clara would not be fooled by such a half-ass effort at concealment. It was all or nothing: either she'd wake and find out, or she'd sleep through the night and have no clue. There was no need to change what was already visible.

Lucy shouldered her backpack and furtively crept across the hardwood floor. She carefully closed the bedroom door behind her.

CHAPTER 3

Lucy had dreamed of the old Sierra Nevada mountain range more times than she could count. She owned a hand-me-down coffee table book with breathtaking black-and-white photographs of clouds over snowcapped crests, a few of which had been taken by the great Ansel Adams himself. Yosemite Valley was included in all its seasonal glory, as well as Sequoia, Kings Canyon, and Devils Postpile. One of the most striking photos was of Lake Tahoe. It was in color and it covered two full pages, the water so blue and serene Lucy felt she could practically put her hand through the picture and dip her fingers in the heavenly paradise.

She returned to that reoccurring fantasy while looking out at the night landscape passing her uncle's truck, her fingers toying with the tiny silver butterfly on a necklace that had been inside the black jewelry box she had taken along. A single quote from John Muir, one of Lucy's Sierra heroes, came to mind:

Everybody needs beauty as well as bread, places to play in and pray in, where nature may heal and give strength to body and soul alike.

She liked to imagine the mountains were exactly the same as when John Muir had seen them, when nature had given him strength and healed his soul. She liked to mentally replace the cemetery of burnt tree stumps that now surrounded both sides of US Highway 395 with flourishing pines and aspens, tall and magnificent, guarding hidden creeks where water flowed in abundance.

It was easy to conjure this fantasy at night. She didn't need to be asleep to pretend.

"You never told me you were lookin' for a hot date tonight."

Lucy turned to Uncle Neil, who stared straight ahead with one hand on the steering wheel and the other scratching an itch beneath the smirk on his face. He wore exactly the same outfit he had been wearing earlier: a grey t-shirt and jeans.

"Ha-ha," Lucy replied, rolling her eyes and taking her fingers off the butterfly. "I'm done with boys for a while, thank you very much."

"Yeah? Since when did you even start with them? Why do I always get left out of this stuff?"

"You didn't miss much. Trust me."

"You girls start younger and younger every year. Hell…when I was your age, I had a boner if I simply brushed a girl's hand by accident."

"Uncle Neil! Gross!"

"What? Just tellin' the truth, Lucy. I didn't have a real girlfriend until my senior year in high school, and even then I was clueless about what to do. I don't think much has changed since then."

They looked at each other for a second, and then laughed.

Lightning flashed on the horizon. They both saw the brief burst, and waited to see if another would follow.

"Rain, finally?" Lucy asked.

"Don't think so," Uncle Neil replied, adjusting his truck's brights. "Saw the same thing last weekend, and ain't nothing come from it. Just passed right over without a single tear for our pain."

"Maybe this time will be different."

"Doubt it," Uncle Neil replied. Then he added, "Who knows. Maybe… So, I hope your aim in all this tonight isn't to sneak a drink or a smoke. Seein' what we do is one thing, but acting like we do is another."

Lucy shook her head. "Nope. I don't want either one of those. Beer is disgusting, and cigarettes are even worse. I'm really glad you don't smoke, Uncle Neil. I don't think I could be around you if you did."

"Good thing you didn't meet me fifteen years ago."

Lucy shot him a surprised glance. "What? You?"

"A bad habit from your grandma. She's not all church sermons and hymns, you know."

"Grandma!"

He pointed a hard finger at Lucy. "Don't you dare go spitting any of this out to her when we get home, you got it? I'll never hear the end of it if you do."

"Of course! I promise."

Uncle Neil held his eyes on Lucy long enough for the vehicle to edge too far over on the shoulder of the road, summoning a clatter of gravel against the undercarriage. He immediately turned back to the highway, straightening their course.

"She smoked because your great-grandpa smoked, and if we follow that line back long enough I'm sure we could find some relatives riding horses with little white sticks juttin' out of their mouths."

"That's no excuse to do it," Lucy replied, watching another bolt of lightning stretch across the horizon in a crescent without ever touching ground.

"I know. But smoking gets you at vulnerable times, kid. Like when you're young and pressured by friends. Or when your boss suddenly tells you to take a vacation and not come back. Or when your brother dies while helping you change a pair of truck tires."

Lucy's mouth opened into a circle. "Uncle Bobby..."

He nodded while switching on the car's left-turn blinker to pass an approaching vehicle crawling along the highway. "That one hit me hard. Never saw it coming, and I would have laughed myself wet had anyone told me it would happen to him. Your Uncle Bobby was so young. So much stronger than I was, even though we did the same tough gigs together."

"If you were twenty-two, then he was twenty, right?"

"Not bad. Pretty good with your math. I guess you aren't cheating on all those school tests you ace after all." He grinned at Lucy; she returned it with a shadow of a smile. "The brain aneurysm killed him before the ambulance even arrived. The day of his funeral, I saw your grandparents smoking on the deck alone. I asked, thinking they'd never let me have one. I even thought I'd hear a few choice curses from Grandpa for being selfish at that time." A dry laugh escaped his throat. "They never said a word. Just handed one over as if we'd been doing that sort of thing for years together."

"Really?"

"Vulnerable times, Lucy. Remember that. It works on those who have been smoking for years, and on those who have never tried it. I know if it had been a different day, an ordinary one, none of that would have happened. I wouldn't have asked, and they sure as shit wouldn't have given it over like a piece of candy."

Lucy stared at the black horizon. The fantasy of the flourishing pines and aspens was now gone. The Sierra Nevada mountains of John Muir and Ansel Adams's day had been replaced by the future the succeeding generations had sowed. The cemetery of burnt trees, though hidden by the night, pressed against the highway and demanded to be felt...to be recognized. The sun's light was not necessary to tell their story. It could be sensed in the lightning igniting behind a curtain of clouds, the desert wind thrusting against their windshield, the dome of distant stars that winked a billion condolences.

Everybody needs beauty as well as bread, places to play in and pray in, where nature may heal and give strength to body and soul alike.

CHAPTER 4

Uncle Neil was the one who had accidently let slip the two facts Lucy knew about her mother. It had happened after a long night of playing cards, and he'd come home after consuming a few too many of his imported liquid luxuries. Lucy, ten at the time, awoke to the sound of arguing. It was three o'clock, and she left her bedroom to check on the commotion, carrying a small bat her late grandpa had given to her in case, in her grandpa's words, an intruder needed convincing to look elsewhere for valuables.

She saw her uncle outside the front door, sitting with his head buried in his hands, Grandma Clara looming over him like a fighter waiting for another knockout.

"Five was the limit, Joe! You swore on my name. How many times do you need to go through this to get it through that rock head of yours? You aren't any good after that, and you know it. Your skills get sloppy. You lose your butt."

"I know, Ma, I know," he replied slowly, struggling to avoid slurring his words. "But I was...I was doin' great, even after that point. Best I've done in weeks."

"What good does that do us when you come home empty-handed, Joe? We don't need to pocket the whole table. I told you what we needed before you left, and you said you'd stop once you got it."

He rocked back on his haunches with his head between his knees. "I didn't want to sleep again, Ma. Not after last night."

"What the heck does that have to do with any of this?"

"I saw Susan, Ma. It was bad. Real, real bad."

20

PART I - FIRE

Grandma Clara shook her head as if looking at a dead rodent that needed to be removed from the house. "You are so piss drunk right now you don't even know what you're saying."

He looked up at her with terrified eyes. "It's true, Ma. Worst nightmare I've ever had. You remember the shackles those animals made her wear? During her whole labor? All eight hours of it? They were in it, Ma! I saw them clear as day!"

She drew in close to him, just inches from his face. "You listen, Joe! You keep those dreams to yourself, you hear? If that little girl sleeping right now gets wind of this, she'll never be the same again. So you just—"

But it was already too late. Both of them turned when the bat Lucy had been holding hit the hardwood floor with a loud thud. It was like the sound of a fist hitting a drum. The bat had just slipped out of Lucy's hands like a wet noodle.

"Lucy!" Grandma Clara shouted, rising and moving to her.

Lucy took off in a flash, bolting up the stairs to her bedroom and locking the door.

Grandma Clara would try for the next thirty minutes to get her to open it, at first using consoling words, then when that failed, trying sharp commands. She finally gave up when she heard Lucy's crying taper off and dissolve into the deep breaths of sleep.

That had been two years ago. The prediction that Uncle Neil's dream would change Lucy held true: she never forgot what she learned that night, and she was determined to get the entire story about her mother, no matter what she had to do to pry it out of the people who knew. Unfortunately, that list of people was very short. Grandma Clara was off limits; Lucy figured she'd have a better chance of drinking a potion and becoming a unicorn than seeing the day when her obdurate grandma finally opened the vault to the past and filled in the missing pieces.

But Uncle Neil was a different story. He had already cracked once, and Lucy had a good feeling he'd do so again if he had the right number of beers and if he felt comfortable enough that he wouldn't face punishment for spilling his secret. Game night satisfied both of those requirements. Lucy's entry in her journal earlier that month documented her arrival at this conclusion:

> *11/2   Need liquor. Would love, love to use*
> *stuff at house, nice and easy, but a bad idea.*
> *Grandma. Always Grandma. Ugh! Must join*
> *him at cards somehow. Plenty of booze from*
> *buddies then. No worrying about sneaking it.*
> *And best of all...no Grandma!*

Lucy hated the manipulation her strategy demanded. She had spent several weeks trying to figure out a better plan without using her uncle, but she failed to find an alternative. Her mother's imprisonment, and whatever crime she'd committed, hadn't been newsworthy to the mainstream media at the time it occurred. Lucy had already tried that sort of general site searching. Asking information from friends of her uncle or grandma was also pointless, because they would just deflect those questions, staying clear of the family matter. Approaching strangers was even worse. She had already heard firsthand the nasty rumors the kids at school had spread, and most of that mendacious information had come from their parents. Lucy was wise enough to know that if there was anything worse than not discovering the truth, it was getting the wrong version of it. She had to have a credible source.

Uncle Neil was her only option.

"What the hell?" came a deep voice from the center of a dimly lit room. Two ceiling fans paddled at thick, stuffy air. A rectangular table stretched beneath the fans: command center for the Saturday night games. "Have you lost your damn mind, Neil?"

"Lord oh lord..." sounded another voice, this one at the opposite end of the long table. A thin haze of cigar smoke softened the aged, wrinkled faces. "What in God's good name is she doing here, Neil?"

Neil led Lucy up to the table as if he hadn't heard a single word or noticed the shock on the many faces. "Fellas, you remember my niece, Lucy.

She's probably shot up like a weed since you've last seen her. But don't any of you old bastards go getting ideas and start hitting on her, or I'll remove the rest of your teeth for you."

"You can't bring her here, Neil," said Pat Day, the owner of the house. His bulky frame engulfed the metal folding chair on which he was sitting—so much so that it looked as if his seat would soon call it quits and collapse under his weight. "This ain't for kids, Neil. Hell, you know that. Your little Lucy's gotta go back home."

"Oh hush, Honey. I'd much rather have her pretty presence than most of the smelly apes around this table, I'll tell you that much."

This voice came from Pat's wife, Helen. She entered the room carrying a tray of freshly baked quesadillas, along with small bowls of sour cream and salsa. She placed the food in the center of group, slapping Pat's hand away as he reached for one.

"Not you, Mr. Diet. Doc said you gotta get that pressure down, and this stuff sure as day won't be taking you in the right direction." Her dirty blonde hair was tied into pigtails. Her face revealed enough wrinkles to give away her age—mid forties—but her body was thin enough to pass for a decade younger. She turned to Lucy. "Take a seat there, sweetie. Move over, Randy and Seth. Make room for Neil, too."

Randy and Seth did as they were told, grumbling in protest as they moved. Though not related, they looked like brothers with their matching bald heads, stocky bodies, and thick mustaches.

"Dear, I really think this is a bad idea. I'm pretty certain Clara didn't give her blessing on this arrangement. Tell me, am I right, Neil?"

Neil opened his mouth to reply, but Helen spoke first. "Oh, I think Clara did, honey. I know sweet Lucy wouldn't be sneaking around like that. Besides, she's here now, and she's our guest to treat right."

Helen glanced at Lucy, throwing her a wink. Lucy smiled nervously, still not sure if she'd be kicked out or not. Her anxiety passed as the men returned to their cards, Pat dealing Neil into their game of Texas Hold'em and telling him the blinds.

"Neil, you lay down another straight flush again this week, I'm checking your damn shirt for tricks," Pat said, taking a puff from his cigar. "How you beat my quads is beyond me."

The corners of Neil's mouth curved as he opened a beer. "I told you to get out on the flop. You can't blame me for riding your horse to the river."

"Ain't nothing in that river, either," Randy said, laughing, the reflection of the ceiling fan light bouncing off his oily head. "Dry as a bone for ya, Pat."

"Not tonight," Pat replied, bending the corners of his two cards so he could see them. His round face betrayed no emotion. "That river will be flowing wild for me."

"Out," Seth said, tossing his cards in the middle.

"Shit, me too," Randy added, no longer laughing. He checked his cards one last time as if they'd somehow change, then flicked them in the same discarded pile.

Lucy ran her tongue over her lips as she stared at the quesadillas in front of her. The delicious smell made her stomach ache.

"Go ahead, sweetie," Helen said, studying Lucy. "I didn't make them as Van Gogh masterpieces to be hanged on the walls."

"Are you sure? I mean, I know how hard dairy is to come by, and I don't want to—"

"Sweetie, I'd much rather see a youthful person like you enjoy these than deal with the heart attacks from these old farts if they got their paws on them."

"Helen baby, words flow like honey from your mouth when you talk like that about us," Randy said, taking a swig from his beer.

"Bout the only thing that's flowing in this room if you get my drift, Randy. Still having a tough time downstairs with the ladies?"

Laughs and whistles from the men exhaled at once. Randy blushed as if he were a little boy, grabbing his beer as a defense and quickly drinking from it.

Lucy giggled, mouth full, a long string of cheese dangling from her lips to the quesadilla in her hand.

"Aren't you going to play, Mrs. Day?" Lucy mumbled.

"You mean join this dreaded headache? Oh no, young lady. Pai gow is my game. I've never had much luck with this one."

"That's because you never gave it a fair shot," Pat said, his eyes on the three flop cards: ten of hearts, queen of spades, five of clubs. "You called it quits after barely two weeks."

"Well, I just didn't like it. What more do you want from me? I have my game, and you have yours."

"Yeah, and at least she wins at hers, Pat," Seth said.

Pat shot Seth a glare, then shifted his eyes across the table. "Well, Neil? You gonna go all in on the first hand?"

Lucy watched her uncle as he thought about his cards for a moment, a swirling line of smoke from Pat's cigar dancing in front of his face...then he slid his cards to the middle of the table, giving in.

"Ha! Not even a second bet! This is going to be easy pickings tonight."

"Evening's young, Patty-O," Neil replied. "Patience is bitter, but its fruit is sweet. Know who said that?"

"As long as your cash keeps ending up in my pocket, Neil, I don't really give a damn who you quote."

Neil glanced at Lucy and gave her a wink. She winked back, but when she tried to smile she realized she had too much of her second quesadilla in her mouth. She knew she looked silly, much like the face of a chipmunk that was stuffed with nuts, and her body shook with laughter.

Pat dealt the next round.

CHAPTER 5

Pat saw the two ladies staring back at him: queen of hearts, queen of clubs. He waited a minute, making a slightly disgruntled face as if given a garbage hand, then raised the bet with an audible grunt—as if he had no choice but to bluff the round.

Inside, he was beaming. This royal pair would not disappoint him. Not this round. He would ride it to the death and wipe that damn smug face off of Neil and send him home penniless.

Randy and Seth quickly folded, a reoccurring theme for them for the past several hours.

Neil glanced at his two hidden cards: seven of hearts, six of clubs. They were much worse than the two cards he'd thrown away during his first hand at the table, but something in his gut told him not to let go of what he had this time. It was a dangerous internal meter. Neil hated to rely on it instead of the cards, because it often let him down, but sometimes it paid off. It was impossible to gauge.

Neil made the call on the bet. Pat dealt the flop—seven of spades, eight of clubs, five of hearts.

It was worthless for Pat, and a twitch at the corner of his mouth revealed his frustration. Randy and Seth, no longer interested in the money that would never flow their way, didn't see it.

But Neil did. It was enough to convince him to keep trusting his inner meter. He checked the bet.

Pat made a continuation bet with his pair, certain Neil would fold again.

Neil called with his pair of sevens, not raising the bet.

Pat laid down a five of spades.

A wide smile creased Pat's face as he glanced at his pair of queens and a pair of fives. "All in," Pat said, pushing his entire cash pile to the center of the table.

The suddenness of the move took Neil by surprise. He was good at calling Pat's bluffs—his friend was a lousy actor—and a quick bet told Neil that Pat had something worthwhile hidden from view. What it was exactly, Neil hadn't the faintest.

"I call," Neil replied. He pushed his cash to the middle, forming a paper mountain. He then flipped over his two cards to reveal his combined pair of sevens.

Pat laughed, showing his two cards. "Two fine ladies to kill your lucky sevens, Neil buddy. Sorry, but this night is gonna end on a sour note for ya."

Neil kept his cool. "Maybe so. It all depends on that river, doesn't it?"

Pat shifted his gaze to the pair of hazel eyes staring at him.

"Please do us the honors, Lady Lucy. I know you must have been bored stiff watching us all this time without playing yourself. Just pick the top one off this stack here, and then you can go home." Pat slid the deck across the table to Lucy.

She shook her head. "Oh no, sir. That's your job. I don't want to make a mistake or something."

"Ain't nothing to it, Lucy. You couldn't mess up if you tried. Go on."

Lucy shifted her eyes to her uncle. He nodded to show that it was okay, even smiled a bit as if he knew whatever she turned would be in his favor. Had Lucy sensed his gut instinct, his internal meter, she wouldn't have had an inch of fear in the world.

Lucy flipped the top card. Four of clubs.

Two fists hit the poker table so hard that the circle of beers jumped a good two inches, with all but one landing safely back down—Randy's can, which was empty anyway and only spilled a few drops on the carpet beside his feet.

"Hell, Pat!" Seth bellowed, lifting his can to his lips to quickly sip the overflowing foam.

"You fucking crazy?" came Randy's voice under the table as he bent to pick up his empty soldier.

"Nobody gets that damn lucky!" Pat screamed across the table, ignoring Seth and Randy. "A straight? Let me guess, did you not play your four aces because they all slipped out of your pockets?"

"Just good karma, Pat. I get it sometimes. Don't know why."

"Karma my fucking ass!"

Pat's voice was now penetrating deep into the house, creating a slight echo. The anger in his tone caused Lucy to stiffen, almost dropping the deck in her hands.

Helen, seated beside her husband with a romance novel in one hand (*Forbidden Longing*), saw Lucy's reaction and immediately put her free hand on Pat's shoulder. "Settle down, dear. No need to blow up about it in front of everyone."

Pat thrust his finger to the middle of the table, pointing at the river card. "Well shit, how else am I supposed to act when we're being cheated right in front of our eyes? You know the damn odds on that showing up like that? Right when he needs it most? Shit...better chance of getting hit by lightning."

Lucy watched her uncle collect his winnings, bunching the cash into two thick stacks, then stand and nod at Helen. He said, "You've been a first-rate host, Mrs. Day. I know I speak for Lucy and myself when I say your cooking and hospitality is second to none."

Helen blushed. "Aww...must you leave now? You barely had one beer, Neil. That's not like you."

Neil waved his hand dismissively at the suggestion. "This uncle has bigger responsibilities. Like getting this young woman back in one piece so I don't end up in pieces myself."

"A wise idea, Neil," Helen replied, opening the front door for them.

"How about just one more round?" Pat asked from the table, now with a forced smile on his face. His round red cheeks couldn't hide the anger still boiling inside. "Got more cash I can get. With that luck of yours, you're bound to do even better."

Neil grinned at Pat. Lucy could tell by the look in her uncle's eyes that there was no way Pat could convince him to stay, not even if a million dollars were piled on the table. "Sorry, buddy. Next time. You can get me then."

Pat's smile instantly vanished. His puffy cheeks somehow managed to become even redder. "To hell with you, Neil! Never come back to this house again! You got me, you bastard!"

Neil chuckled and exited the house. Lucy quickly followed him, unaccustomed to such outbursts and not knowing if this exchange was one of many her uncle had experienced while playing cards, or if it was something rare and personal. She didn't want to stay to find out.

CHAPTER 6

Neil was tired, but he didn't need to activate the auto-driver navigation system to guide the truck back home, as he often did after his late-night card games. He didn't quite trust it with Lucy in the vehicle. The feature was perfectly safe (it had gotten him home without problems hundreds of times), but he wanted his own two hands on the wheel just to make sure.

Lucy wasn't surprised. She recalled her uncle telling Helen about not wanting Grandma Clara to tear him to pieces. She would have even found his caution amusing, had she not been disappointed by the fact that her goal for the night would now never be achieved. There was zero chance he would offer any insightful information about her mother. Not now. Not while he was as sober as a watchdog, staring intently at the highway lane lines streaming past them like yellow bullets.

She considered giving it a shot anyway. He'd had a wonderful night, winning big, and maybe in his good mood he'd reveal one last hand—cards he'd secreted away ever since Lucy was a baby. Lucy could deal the river. She could casually start a conversation about how the boys at school still teased her about her past, and subtly steer that topic toward the night she heard her uncle talk about his nightmare. Lucy could lay out all the cards and let her uncle join right in, finally ending the game she no longer wanted to play. It was still feasible, she thought. It was just the two of them on a lone highway, late in the night with lightning still igniting the thirsty land, and her uncle just might feel comfortable enough to play along.

But Lucy held back.

Part of her reticence had to do with the fear of screwing her chances of ever finding out if her ruse failed. If he said no tonight, his guard would be up on the subject. Lucy would find herself facing a thicker and higher wall the next time around. It would be near impossible to pry his secret loose.

But another part of it had to do with not wanting to manipulate her uncle and to just enjoy herself—to let the night unfold without trying to control it. She had felt like an adult at the poker table. She never played a single hand during the game (declining Helen's invitations a few times), and yet she'd still felt like she fit in with the group. It had been a thrilling sensation. The men didn't hold back their curses or crude jokes or outbursts in her presence, which had been a surprise given their initial hesitations of having her at the table.

Inquiring about her mother now, Lucy felt, would tarnish the atmosphere of the evening. She wanted to savor this experience. The night was perfect just the way it was, and Lucy was content to keep her past in the dark for a bit longer.

She figured the opportunity would present itself again, especially since she'd left a good impression, so why rush it? It didn't have to be tonight.

CHAPTER 7

Lucy and her uncle swore they had pulled it off. All windows at the front of the house were still black when Neil pulled the truck to a stop in the driveway, and the same darkness and silence permeated the house as they entered through the back door and crept up the stairs. Lucy's bedroom door was shut, and the same was true for the doors to her uncle and grandma's rooms—all positive signs pointing to a success.

But the truth hit them like a jolt to the stomach.

As soon as her uncle whispered goodnight, yawning and making his way to his room, Lucy slipped off her shoes and slid into her bed without realizing that someone was waiting in the shadows just a few feet away. Had Lucy's eyes adjusted to the darkness of her room in time, she would have seen the figure sitting in her desk chair—a ghostly mass facing directly toward the bed. Lucy would have seen it slowly rise, advance a step, and reach for another dark object on the desk.

Lucy's eyes immediately shot open as the light hit her face like a slap. Her body jolted forward, a scream tearing up her throat like a startled animal, halting at the edge of her mouth only upon seeing the one face that shocked her into silence.

"Tell me, was it fun tonight, Lucy-Lu? A real blast?"

Lucy scrambled for a reply, her mind swirling as if she'd just gotten off an amusement park ride. "Grandma..." It was all she could summon.

"So...did it work? Your little trick tonight?"

Lucy's eyes leapt to the journal in her grandma's left hand. She had forgotten all about it when she'd gotten into bed—never noticing its absence from the top cover where she had placed it before going out.

Under different circumstances, Lucy would have been mad as hell at anyone sneaking a peek at it. But she had dug her own hole tonight. Shifting from shock to rage was not a wise decision.

"Grandma, I didn't ask Uncle Neil any of what I wrote in that! I promise, not once!"

"Mom!"

They both turned to the open bedroom door, where Neil stood in black boxers and a ratty white undershirt. His face looked boyish at that moment—mouth agape, eyes wide, forehead stretched back.

"Joe, I will talk to you in the morning! Get on to bed now!"

Neil either didn't hear her or underestimated her determination. He stepped forward. "Mom, it was my fault. Don't blame this on Lucy. I agreed to the whole thing when I could have easily said no. This is on my head, so don't—"

"Enough! You let us be, Joe! Damn it, let us be!"

Lucy watched in fear as her grandma straightened her posture and narrowed her eyes in rage. It was the first time she had heard her grandma swear. Her grey hair was no longer in the bun she often kept it in; it fell around her wrinkled face like dangling strands of a dry mop. Her lips were pressed together in a thin line. Her cheeks were a bruised red.

Lucy's uncle opened his mouth to say more, but his tongue remained still in the fury of the moment. This wasn't Patrick Day with whom he was dealing. That argument had been a comic play—one that would soon be forgotten when the next weekend rolled around and new money was laid on the table.

"Back to your room, Joe," Grandma Clara said, as if he were a boy again. Her eyes remained fixed on his until he dropped his gaze and made his way back. She remained quiet until she heard his bedroom door close, then turned to Lucy.

33

"Grandma, I swear I didn't ask Uncle Neil about my mom," Lucy fired, rushing the words out before more harm could be done. "Everything went wrong, and I knew he wouldn't say anything anyway. And now I know not to do it at all. I'll rip those stupid pages out of my diary and burn them."

Grandma Clara slowly walked to Lucy's bedroom window. Flashes of lightning hit her worn, hunched body like bursts from a strobe light, half-concealing her face in the grey mop of her hair.

"Grandma?" Lucy asked at length, her heart racing faster. The deathly silence was far worse than a verbal lashing.

"It's time you know, child."

"What?"

Her grandma faced her with eyes that were as dark as the seed of midnight. It took everything in Lucy's power not to hide from that look...not to seek protection under her covers.

"I figured this day would come. I was hoping it was a lot farther on the horizon when I'd be more prepared, or at least less reluctant to tell you. Half of me even thought it might not be necessary, Lucy-Lu. That you'd somehow get all the pieces you needed from others, and that in itself would be enough. It was foolish, wishful thinking."

Lucy's heart was now beating hard in her throat. She found herself shaking her head uncontrollably from side to side.

"No, Grandma. Huh-uh. I don't want to know what happened now. I don't care anymore. It doesn't matter."

She watched as her grandma slowly moved back, sat beside her, and placed a hand on her trembling fingers. Her grandma's hands were warm, while her own were icy—as if she'd been rolling snowballs.

"Yes, Lucy-Lu. You do. No more with this hiding."

A tear rolled down Lucy's cheek as her gaze met her grandma's. Her black eyes were now a deep, warm blue.

"Grandma..."

"It's time, sweetie."

CHAPTER 8

The hot cup of tea in Lucy's hands felt comforting. It was orange spice, her favorite, and the temperature was just right—it hadn't been on the stove long enough to scald her fingers or lips. It had been a while since she'd last had it, and the taste still reminded her of birthdays and holidays, when there was always a full pot of it on the dinner table.

Now seated in the same wicker swing her uncle had been rocking in earlier that afternoon—which now seemed like a year ago—Lucy swayed gently with her eyes fixed on the liquid in her cup. Grandma Clara sat across from her, in a chair she had taken from the kitchen. She too had a cup of hot tea in her hands—Earl Gray.

"Your mom loved the movies, Lucy-Lu. I'm not talking about the new stuff, with all that dang violence and terrible language. She was a classics junky. Gone with the Wind. Lawrence of Arabia. Rebel without a Cause. Rear Window. Practically all the silver screen greats, from when movie-making was still just a baby."

She took a sip of her tea and watched as a long stretch of lightning split the sky, then vanished. No thunder accompanied it.

"There used to be a theater not far down the main highway. They'd play those old films for close to nothing, and your mother was probably the only reason they stayed afloat for as long as they did. She was there just about every Saturday night, sometimes with friends, sometimes alone if she couldn't find anyone to tag along." Lucy's grandma laughed, revealing deep wrinkles at the corners of her eyes and mouth. "Susan even tried to get me to go on those lonely nights. I usually had things to do with your grandpa or odd jobs around the house, but on occasion I'd break away from those obligations and join her because I liked those movies too. Not as much as your mom did, of course, but enough to look forward to it when driving to the theater."

Her gaze lowered from the pyrotechnics of the storm to the dusty wooden porch floor. Her face seemed to slump as her eyes dropped.

"I wish I would have joined her more often," she said in a voice so soft Lucy barely heard the words. "Life is filled with so much unnecessary busyness, child. So much bullshit occupies our time that we fail to see the moments that really matter. The moments of love and appreciation for the rare gifts in our lives that will someday pass."

Lucy's eyes widened upon hearing a second curse out of her grandma. She was starting to see the real Clara Beth Gold, the woman who had witnessed decades of the world's naked nature, acquiring wisdom at every step of her journey. Gone was the caricature "grandma" role Lucy had given her. This was the bare Clara—her defenses down, her self-imposed parental limitations stripped away.

"One night Susan went to the theater alone to see Citizen Kane. Seated behind her was a man named Ted Burrows, who was with a buddy who had dragged him to the movie. Susan had to tell Ted half a dozen times to shut his nasty mouth during the film. She said he kept cracking crude jokes about the characters and scenes. His buddy was no better. His whole reason for taking Ted was to make a big mockery out of the experience, picking on the audience as much as what they saw on the screen. It pissed Susan off something awful. She confronted Ted and his friend after the showing, threatening to force them to pay everyone back their ticket price because of what they had done. The theater manager had to step in and break up the fight, ordering Susan and the two men outside."

"But she didn't do anything," Lucy replied, hands curled around the tea mug. "It was them, not her."

Lucy's grandma nodded. "I know. I wish that manager never would have done that. A bloody fight would have been far better than what eventually happened to your mother."

"What do you mean?" Lucy asked.

"Out in the parking lot, Ted switched on his charm. Your mother was a very pretty girl, just like you, and unfortunately Ted had enough in the looks department to interest her, even though she still wanted to punch his face in. She had a weakness for bad boys, I guess. She was young, and a lot of girls go through that stage before realizing those types of relationships always lead to the same destination: heartbreak hill."

"Not me," Lucy said with a fierce determination in her eyes. "I'm not scared of being alone forever, if it comes to that. I'll never fall for jerks like that."

Grandma Clara smiled. "I believe you are right, Lucy-Lu. You are very mature for your age. An old soul, as they say. Anyway, Ted made a half-assed apology to your mother for the incident and told her he'd make it up by buying her dinner at CJ's Eats, a diner that is now nothing but broken windows and graffiti-tagged bricks. It was a nice place at the time. Your grandpa took me there a few times for anniversaries. Ted was the only child of an alcoholic father and an inept mother, and how he got the money to afford such a place has always been a great mystery to me. Regardless, he coughed up the cash and wooed your mother right onto his hook."

"Yuck," Lucy said, putting a finger inside her mouth to show her disgust. "How could she fall for that creep?"

"Love is a powerful force, sweetie. It drowns logic and traps the heart in a sea of emotion. You have to experience it firsthand to truly appreciate the firmness of its grip on human actions. I had it with your grandpa very early on. I couldn't stop thinking about him when he was away. It was as if all memories had been wiped clean, and everything in my life revolved around his next visit or our scheduled dates."

"But Grandpa was nice."

"Yes. I got lucky. Your mother, not so much. In fact, she couldn't have picked a worse partner to fall for. It wasn't long after she started dating Ted that his abusive nature started to show. He'd ridicule her in public, calling her nasty names. He'd put her down just to raise himself up a few inches, mocking her accomplishments, belittling her dreams, criticizing her every move. I'm not sure what I hated more, his foul mouth or his fists."

"You mean he hit her?" Lucy asked with shock.

Her grandma nodded somberly. "That came when they moved in together, about five months into their relationship—if such a word can even be used for that terrible time they spent together. It started with small bruises on her neck and arms. Quarter-sized. Sometimes larger. Purple or light black. I didn't think much of them at first because your mother was pretty good at concealing them with makeup or clothes, and she was always doing manual work in the garden and around the house, an excuse she used a few times when a bruise was just too large or bright to hide. I remember asking about one of them. It was an oval-shaped dark patch on her right shoulder. She told a clever story about planting a pear tree in their backyard...that she'd had to use her weight to hoist it at a proper angle so it could be set right. It was a clever cover story because part of it was based on fact. I had seen that very tree in their yard not long after they'd planted it, and it was large enough to make me wonder how they'd even transported the thing from the nursery in Ted's small pickup."

"Yeah, but you caught on."

"As it always goes with such awful behavior, yes. It got out of her control. Black eyes. Bloody, fat lips. Fractured ribs. He was a monster, and deep inside she knew he'd always be that way no matter how charming he was the following day, with his lies and excuses as to why he had done what he did."

"Why didn't she go to the police? Or just leave that creep? It wasn't as if she was married to him."

Lucy's grandma turned to the pyrotechnics of the storm. Flashes from the lightning illuminated her in sporadic bursts, throwing a flickering dark shadow of her figure down the length of the wooden porch all the way to the screen backdoor.

"Fear ruins lives, child. You cannot think rationally when paralyzed by fatalistic thoughts of your current situation. Outside opinions take second priority. By the time the evidence of the physical abuse on her body started to

39

manifest clearly to the outside world, the fear of leaving him had already soaked her to her marrow. She was terrified of taking action against him. She had already lost one baby to his rage; she was horrified of losing another."

Lucy's head shot back in shock. "Huh? Baby?" That one word sent shivers from the nape of her neck to her feet, and a heavy wave of dread crashed down upon her.

Grandma Clara fixed her gaze on Lucy, staring with the same dark eyes that she had shown by the bedroom window. She nodded in regret. "A sister, Lucy-Lu. You had an older sister. To be honest, you two could never have existed in this world at the same time; her absence paved the way for your conception. But I still consider her a sibling because your mother would have brought her to full term had it not been for Ted."

"What do you mean, Grandma?"

"Susan became pregnant shortly after moving in with him. As I mentioned, she was good at keeping secrets. It took two and a half months for her to finally tell me about her pregnancy, and she only did because she knew she'd have no choice but to reveal the truth in the trimesters ahead. An expanding belly is rather hard to hide. She told me in her backyard, while we were watching the spring heat bake the dickens out of that pear tree. The few winter blossoms on that tree had dried to a crisp. Standing not far from it, Susan caught me off guard with a sudden fierce hug that took the wind out of me and almost caused me to tip over like a bottle. She let her secret free. She had tears in her eyes, a river of them, and I knew in that instant that she hadn't told Ted for fear of how he would respond. I told her to immediately leave him. Begged her to. She said she would, but I could tell by the way she was holding me that her mind still wasn't made up. It wasn't just fright. At the time, she still had a faint flicker of hope that a baby could somehow tame his violent nature and bring love into their house. She was still blinded by his damn charm. She felt a child could bring some amount of normalcy to their lives, and do what she couldn't do herself."

"A sister..." Lucy said, shaking her head, still in shock. "An older sister."

"One that was beaten out of your mother. That beast of a man got fired from his job one night and came home drunk, pouring his rage out on Susan. She tried to stop the blows by revealing her pregnancy, but that only made the situation worse. He focused his kicks and punches on her stomach. Told her he'd have no bastard child living in his house. He wailed on her until she bled top and bottom—in her mouth, between her legs. How she escaped with her own life that night is something of a miracle. But the baby wasn't as lucky."

"He killed it," Lucy said in a low whisper.

"Forced a miscarriage. Susan said when he was using the restroom, she fled out the back door, ran to her car, and sped away. It was while she was driving that it happened. She told me she felt terrible cramps about halfway between her house and mine. Fearing the danger in pulling over, having no idea if Ted was driving after her, she pushed herself to deal with the pain until she knew she was a safe distance away. That meant being with me. When I opened the front door, I could barely recognize her. Her face was as swollen as a pumpkin, and her hair and hands were caked in dried blood. She looked like some creature from a horror film, and if it wasn't for her voice I'm not sure I would have kept that door open as long as I did. 'Mommy,' she said, crying. She was a child in that moment. A scared, battered girl who'd been through the devil's den and needed a mother's love and protection. She collapsed in my arms and sobbed in a way that shook me to my center. It still gives me chills even now...just thinking of her crying like that."

Lucy's grandma stopped for a moment, taking a sip of her tea and looking off in the black void of the night. The distant sound of thunder rumbled from the edge of the hidden horizon. "That night she finally agreed to leave him once and for all, but I couldn't convince her to report what had happened to the police. That is one of my biggest regrets... Had we filed the proper paperwork, we could have prepared for what came next. Perhaps even have prevented it."

"What, Grandma?" Lucy asked. "What do you mean by next? You said she left him."

"The forced miscarriage flipped a switch in Susan. That little girl who had stood in the doorway with blood all over her...well, she quickly transformed into a woman bent on justice for her baby. As her face and body healed from the blows, her internal emotional wounds just grew worse. Infected the mind, you could say. She clearly saw the monster who had been her lover, and I think she had serious fears that if given the opportunity, he'd either come after her again or hurt someone in her family."

"Uncle Neil would've knocked the lights out of that dummy. One-handed."

"Maybe so, Lucy-Lu. But that wasn't the kind of justice your mother needed. Like you and your journal, she was good at making plans when she set her mind to it. Your mother could keep it all in her head, though. That's what made her so good at keeping secrets. She was smart, a hell of a lot brighter than most people gave her credit for, and she kept all thoughts to herself regarding the details of how she'd pay Ted back for what he did."

"Sweet revenge on that creep," Lucy said with a thin smile. "I love it."

"Don't you say that, Lucy!" Grandma Clara blasted at her. Her voice was almost a shout, and the strength of her anger made Lucy flinch. "It's the worst part of human nature. Men seeking men to deliver vengeance greater than the injustice that was delivered upon them. It never ends. True strength, true love is in mercy. Forgiveness is the core of human growth, and it can only be achieved by accepting the difficult terms of its agreement. No matter what someone has done to you, you have to use compassion to fight the evil, and find room in your heart to walk away without lashing out. I cannot begin to tell you how hard that is. I've met some people in my life who were real pieces of work...the kind who contributed absolutely nothing to the grand picture of human advancement. You could even say they detracted from it. I loathed them. I wanted to wipe their nasty existence off this world and erase the harmful memories they'd created in every person they'd encountered. But that begets more nastiness, child. It only leads to more pain and tears."

"Even with Ted?" Lucy asked. "You can't tell me you found mercy for that creep."

"Even Ted, Lucy-Lu. He had a terrible past that was never revealed to us. Since then I've heard a few rumors about his upbringing, nothing I want to get into now, but I'm fairly sure most of the rumors were true because of his dark nature. I'm not saying this to justify his actions. I believe in responsibility and accountability, just like your uncle does. Maybe even more so. I just come from the school of thought that mercy is the only path to true healing. Without it, the wounds never seal."

"Did Mom's seal?" Lucy asked, already guessing the answer.

Grandma Clara shook her head and remained silent for a minute. More thunder hammered the parched land. "She did what she felt she needed to do. About five weeks after that miscarriage, she answered one of his phone calls. He'd been trying her cell at least twice a day all during that time. Sometimes he'd leave sweet messages, saying how much he missed and loved her. Sometimes he'd be drunk and horny and just wanted a lay. Sometimes he'd drunkenly release his rage in long-winded rants. My math fails me when I try to add up the total of the messages he'd left for her."

A faint rustling sounded from inside the house. Grandma Clara looked toward the noise, Lucy following her gaze, but nothing stirred. All windows were dark.

Grandma Clara continued, "She told him she was going to drive over so they could talk and work things out. Ted must have had to try with all his might to prevent himself from dropping the phone upon hearing her words. Susan hadn't said a single word to him since they parted. Of course, Ted would have dropped that phone and gotten the hell out of that house had he known Susan's true reason for coming over. She had no intention of patching things up and putting up with more of his crap."

"What did she do?"

Lucy's grandma stared deep into her eyes, searching Lucy with a reluctant gloom. It was as if the eyes looking at Lucy belonged to Susan, and she was testing the strength of her child. Seeing if she was old enough. Ready enough.

Grandma Clara sighed, forcing herself to continue. "Your mother had sex with Ted for the last time that day. When she first arrived at the house, they did a small amount of talking in the kitchen...enough to satisfy Ted that she was considering coming back, and enough not to tip him off that she had ulterior motives. Susan wore a revealing blouse, knowing Ted would be sexually frustrated and go after her at the first chance he could get. Your mother told me they did the deed in the bedroom. It was the hardest thing for her to do, she said. She absolutely hated him to the root, and found him so repulsive that she threw up not long after he finished, while he was in the shower. She was outside when her stomach let go. Susan said she was so nervous at that moment she felt she was going to faint, or die of a heart attack. She said her plan would've completely failed if he didn't do his regular routine; everything depended on it."

Lucy shot her grandma a puzzled look.

"Susan explained that Ted always took a shower after they had sex. He felt the need to wash himself off for some strange reason, and spent at least ten to fifteen minutes soaking himself in hot water."

"But how? The smart pours cut us off after two minutes. Any longer is illegal."

"It used to be eight minutes back then, before they changed the rule yet again and made things much harder for us. What Ted did was still illegal even in those days, but he had the same regard for the law as he did for human decency. He somehow rigged the tub the way he wanted it to get more water. Anyway, Susan said her life was banking on him taking that shower, and she said he didn't go in at first. He stayed on the bed for a while, talking about what a great lay she was and how he wanted to do her again in the night. He even had the nerve to tell her that she needed to lose a few pounds around the thighs to make her even better. Susan said she thought he'd never leave—that he would just jabber away until her opportunity slipped by. But as I said, that didn't happen. He got in the bathroom, and she rushed out. The minute she lost while throwing up was the climax of her nervousness. She said it felt like she had lost an hour in that moment, and that she was terrified she'd see Ted burst out of the house with his fists clenched and his mouth firing curses. She quickly regained her composure, opened the trunk to her car, and got out a five-gallon gasoline can along with a long lighter."

"Grandma..." Lucy said with wide eyes, knowing where the story was leading.

"She doused the bedroom first, soaking the queen mattress where so many nightmares had occurred, then she moved on to the hallway. She splashed gasoline on the walls, floor, and doors, including the ajar bathroom door, which had steam pouring out in wispy clouds. Susan said she was most worried about the smell. It reeked to high heaven, the fumes burning her nose. As she worked further into the house, she imagined Ted finally getting a whiff of the odor, killing the shower faucet, and swiftly exiting the bathroom to catch her in the act. That's what she pictured over and over again in her mind, even as she exited the house and made a liquid line from the front door all the way to the mailbox at the street curb."

"He never came out?"

"He did, but not at first. Susan said her hands were shaking so hard she had no idea how she managed to work the lighter. She dropped it twice. On the third attempt, it lit and the trail she created to the house soon became a growing sliver of fire. It worked quickly down the damp path, entering the front door like a snake from hell, then everything became eerily silent. Susan told me her heart froze in her chest. She thought she'd made a mistake...that the fire hadn't caught all the way, that it had stopped about halfway in. She remembered seeing a raven land on top of the house right at that moment while she was waiting beside the mailbox with her knees in the dirt. Strange thing to recall, I suppose, considering the circumstances. But that bird is what tipped her off that there was no mistake. It suddenly took flight as the whole house seemed to heave. The flames had found every drop of the gas she'd left. Smoke started to pour out the front door, and then out of unseen crevices in the roof. A tongue of fire licked out the open door, and continued to do so as a grey plume swelled up into the blue sky, eventually blocking out the afternoon sun. Susan retained every detail of that day. She said it was like a movie in her mind that kept repeating over and over."

"But it didn't work. She only burned the house, since he got out."

"That's not what I told you, sweetie. It's true a living creature exited that house. Whether it was a man, or the scorched remains of the demon that had possessed that man, only the good Lord knows. It came crashing through a window about ten feet from the front door. It was engulfed in flames from its feet to its singed, blackened head. Deafening screams bellowed out of it like a burning devil as it fell to the front porch floor along with a rain of glass fragments. It twitched and flopped while the fire did its work, eating the fuel that was his flesh. It frightened me out of my wits to hear Susan tell this story, especially the part when she said she had a brief urge to put the flames out. 'It was instinct to help a person in danger, but I just let it pass,' she said, utterly indifferent. Her instincts did pass, but not before Ted's final gaze fell upon her. His eyes were filled with shock and fear. It was as if he knew what lay in store for him when he crossed to the other side, the eternal one, and he was reacting to the improbable fact that the one person who had forced him into that dark world was the battered woman whom he'd controlled for so long. Susan must have seemed like the Grim Reaper to him in that fleeting moment. She'd brought death to his door at the unlikeliest hour, and no mercy would flow from her hardened heart. He knew she would just sit and watch him burn. And that's just what she did. She stared until the house came crumbling down, burying him in a fiery grave."

Grandma Clara took the last few sips of her tea.

Lucy stared at her in stunned silence. She couldn't picture her mother going through all of that, doing all of that, the entire appalling experience compressed into a single day. Her grandma was right about what she said earlier: it was like something out of a horror movie. Lucy couldn't fathom that it was a part of *her* family past, and for the first time in her life, she understood why the truth had been hidden from her for so long.

"There's more, I'm afraid," Grandma Clara said, following two loud cracks of thunder.

Lucy shook her head. "I don't want to hear anymore. I know that creep was my father. If that's the last big secret, you don't have to worry about telling me. I figured that out on my own. Hard not to, since it explains why he's never around now."

Lucy's grandma got up and sat next to her on the wicker swing. She put a consoling hand on Lucy's shoulder. "You're a smart girl, but what I have to say isn't about Ted being your father. It's what happened to your mom. She drove to the police station that very day and turned herself in. She told them everything, all the nasty details. Some of what I've told you earlier actually came from the police report itself, when it was read in court as evidence during her trial. The district attorney treated her like a remorseless criminal. He charged her with first-degree premeditated murder, and wanted the maximum sentence. The trial lasted just four days, a blink on the docket schedule considering how most murder cases drag on for weeks…but your mother made it easy for them. Going against the advice of her defense attorney, she confessed to everything in the police report and bravely faced the punishment for her crime. She might have gotten a favorable sentence had the circumstances of the offense been a little easier to swallow. But the killing was just too grisly, and the DA got what he wanted. She received thirty years to life, and was sentenced to spend her time at the Mammoth State Penitentiary, a few hours north of here."

"She's still there? You mean my mom's been that close to me all this time and I didn't even know it?"

Grandma Clara diverted her gaze away from Lucy. "She wasn't there long, sweetie. She gave birth to you several months in. I had thought every county in California had long ago outlawed restraints during labor, but I found out differently on the day your eyes opened for the first time. They had tied and chained her like some sort of wild animal, claiming she was a danger to the physician and medical staff. It made me mad as hell. I later found out that it was illegal, but I didn't know that at the time. I'll never know how she summoned the courage and strength to go through that kind of delivery; it was a testament to her remarkable willpower, an inner vigor that I've never seen the likes of before or since. She spiritually removed herself from those shackles. She wanted you to live, to have the life your sister didn't, and she poured all her energy into that purpose until you were safely out and breathing."

"That's how she died. Giving birth to me…"

"No. She survived that." Grandma Clara sighed, long and deep. "She was fatally stabbed in the prison cafeteria just a few weeks after you were born. The warden released a statement claiming that the killing was the result of a fight between Susan and another prisoner over contraband. They quickly dismissed it as a drug-related skirmish. But that was all nonsense. Susan never touched any substance that messed with her mind or body, not even during delivery, when an epidural was available to her in spite of her restraints. The knife itself was the only contraband they should have been focusing on. That prisoner had been bribed and given that weapon from someone on the outside. I have no idea who, but I'll go to my grave knowing in my heart that a friend or family member of Ted's arranged the murder. It was no damn jail scuffle."

A tear streamed down Lucy's face. Another one followed. "I'm sorry, Grandma. I'm so, so sorry."

Grandma Clara took Lucy in her arms and held her tightly.

"Oh sweetheart, why are you apologizing? What have *you* done?"

"You wanted to keep this awful story away from me. Now I know why. I was so dumb tonight, Grandma. I, I, I..." Lucy tried to stammer out her thoughts, but she broke down, sobbing with all her body, shaking the swing. She wailed in her grandma's arms while thunder cracked overhead. The smell of ozone was thick in the wind.

After letting it all out, she raised her wet, puffed face and stared right into the aged eyes watching her. "I love you, Grandma."

"I know you do, Lucy-Lu. And I love you with all my heart and soul." She gave Lucy a tight squeeze, kissing her forehead as she did so. "The same was true with your mother. I recognized it in her eyes when she saw you for the first time. She had so much love to give the world, and I think it's now passed on to you. It's a part of your unique destiny. Be a light of mercy and forgiveness. Be a beacon of compassion and healing in all that you do with your life."

They stared at each other for a long moment, then turned toward the house upon hearing more rustling.

"Oh Neil... Just get your butt out here already. You're not fooling anybody with all that racket."

After a minute, the screen door slowly opened. Out poked Neil's head. "Who? Me?"

The silly reply to Grandma Clara's order and the sight of his surprised face made Lucy's sorrow instantly vanish. Streams of tears were still fresh on her cheeks, but she laughed like she'd never laughed before in her life.

Grandma Clara joined her, throwing her head back and cackling.

Neil frowned, not understanding the joke, and came out to join them. He moved to the edge of the porch and stretched out his hand. He had to wait for a few seconds, but he confirmed what he thought he'd seen against the whiteness of the flashing lightning. "Rain! It's rain!"

Without saying a word, Lucy and her grandma got off the swing and walked to where he was standing. They put their hands out in the same manner, standing side by side, feeling tiny drops on their fingers and palms.

"He's right, Grandma!" Lucy repeated with a wide smile. "Rain!"

Grandma Clara nodded, shocked. "By the grace of God, it is. I can't believe it."

The drizzle quickly turned into a downpour, and Neil jumped down from the porch and danced in the deluge. Lucy immediately followed him, laughing with glee.

"Come on, Mom!" Neil said, waving her over. "Get out here!"

"Oh stop," Grandma Clara replied shyly. "I'm too old for that."

"Come on!" Lucy echoed. "All of us!"

Grandma Clara chuckled at the thought, shook her head, and slowly let herself down, joining them. The three generations linked hands, dancing in a circle. The thunder provided the beat, the rain the melody. It was nature's long-missed harmony—the purest music ever composed.

PART II
WATER

CHAPTER 9

It was a hell of a way for Lucy to celebrate her 24th birthday. She was up to her chin in funky water that smelled like a mixture of sewage and mold, unable to see where she was wading in it and certain she'd soon find her legs shredded by a jagged piece of glass or punctured by one of the orphanage's displaced wrought iron railings. Blackness filled her eyes. Her flashlight had shorted out several hours ago, and her waterproof flare was out of the question given the risk of gas leaks.

"Is anybody in here?" Lucy asked, slogging forward inch by miserable inch. "Say something if you can hear me."

A faint noise drifted toward her from the dank darkness. It sounded like a voice, but Lucy couldn't tell with certainty. Everything that reached her ears on this chaotic day seemed like someone calling for help. Her mind couldn't distinguish where fantasy stopped and the nightmare of this reality started.

"Adam, this is Lucy," Lucy said into a small handheld radio transceiver. "Are you getting this message?"

She waited and listened. All that came through was the same static she'd been hearing for the past several hours.

The water was warm and thick. It felt exactly as Lucy had been told it would feel just before she'd exited the transport helicopter: *"Just one endless summer swamp down there. Revenge of Louisiana's wetlands. Ain't anything Big Easy about it, so all of you birds be careful and look out."*

That advice had come from Captain Conner Wells, one of the most experienced pilots in Rescue Ravens, an international first-aid organization dedicated to helping the communities hit hardest by global coastal flooding. Lucy had known Conner for over two years. He was the first pilot Lucy was assigned to when she volunteered for the Rescue Ravens ground support division, and, by luck, the only one she'd ever had to count on to get her safely to and from the target sites. They were three for three so far: Miami, Pensacola, and Galveston. The current mission, the Garden District of New Orleans, was threatening to shatter that perfect record. Barely six hours into their mission, Lucy had already lost contact with Conner; Director Jamie Price, the ground division leader; and all three members of her rescue team— including Adam, owner and operator of the dinghy they'd used to get to the orphanage.

Like the Big Easy itself, the operation had turned into a chaotic, deadly mess. Reaching anyone via phone or text was an impossibility, since the city's communication towers had been knocked out after the first levee failure. Her handheld transceiver was her only method of outside contact.

"Heeelloooo? Is anyone in here? Do you need help?"

Lucy blindly waded another two steps before feeling something slimy brush her hand. She gently closed her fingers around it, then immediately let go, positive she had grabbed a snake. She froze in the stagnant water, barely breathing. Nothing stirred. She reached out again, slowly, and felt the slick skin floating in front of her path. It wasn't a snake; it was a human body.

Chapter 10

"Damn," Lucy said, pulling the arm toward her so she could check the pulse to confirm what she already suspected.

Enveloped in darkness, she felt the wrist, then the neck. Nothing beat against her finger. Moving to the delicate features of the face, she guessed the age of the dead orphan to be about five or six. Long, tangled hair floated aimlessly around the skull, eternally anchoring it in place and revealing the child's gender: female.

Lucy sighed, shook her head, and gently pushed the body aside. She continued on, praying others weren't beyond hope.

"Please say something if you need help! I'm not here to hurt you. Is anyone here?"

"Yes..."

Lucy halted her advance. It was the same voice she thought she'd heard earlier. It was very soft, but this time the word *yes* had been unmistakable. It wasn't just her mind playing tricks; a child was alive somewhere in the ruins of the St. Charles Orphanage, most likely deathly weak and frightened after surviving for five days in such wretched conditions.

"Where are you?" Lucy asked, moving forward slowly, not knowing if the voice had come from behind or in front.

She was on the orphanage's second floor, deep in the middle of a long hallway that stretched the length to four bedrooms and two half-bathrooms. The building, or what was left of it, was a Victorian style three-story house that the city of New Orleans had designated as a historic structure back in 1926. Lucy had seen the commemorative metal plaque when Adam threaded their dinghy between two pillars at the front gate. The original owners had put the sign about head high, around five feet up from the sidewalk. The height of the flood had touched the bottom of the plaque.

Lucy knew that the plaque was now well submerged. Another levee had breached shortly after Adam had dropped her off three hours ago, pouring more water into an already devastated city.

"Keep talking to me! I cannot see anything. I need to hear you to help."

She carefully dragged one foot in front of the other, keeping her chin up to avoid the water entering into her mouth. Her biggest worry was another levee failure. Only a few feet of breathable air stood between the ceiling and her chin. If the height of the flood rose again like it had earlier, Lucy—and any children still alive in the house—would meet an unpleasant end, drowning like mice on a doomed vessel.

"Please...say something. I need your voice to guide me."

Lucy's hand touched another slick object. It was round, just like the wrist she had felt moments ago, and she immediately assumed with dread and resignation that she had stumbled into another young victim.

She breathed out in relief when she felt the hardness of the material, and the cross sections of identical texture. It was a chair.

"Oh thank God," Lucy said, pushing it aside.

"This way. I'm over here."

Lucy barely caught the voice over her own. She reminded herself to keep her trap shut when being forced to rely solely on her ears to find her path.

She was fairly certain this time that the voice had come from in front of her, not behind. She quickened her pace. The increase didn't amount to much, given the circumstances, but it was better than lollygagging around when her life—and the life of whoever was calling for her—depended on getting out before more levees folded under the weight of mankind's carelessness. Nature had another lesson to teach, but Lucy had been to more than her fair share of those lessons in California and had every intention of sitting the next few out.

"Am I close?" Lucy asked, feeling the hallway walls, hoping to find a door that, once opened, would allow outside light to penetrate the black void swallowing her. "Are you in a room?"

"Yes," came the voice. "In here."

A boy, Lucy thought. She was close enough to make the determination from the tone of his voice, and placed his age between five and seven. His voice carried his fear. It was shaky, not quite desperate, but not far from it, either.

"Keep talking to me, please. It really helps. My name is Lucy. What's yours?"

More wading. More blind groping down a corridor wall already slimy with the onset of mold and mildew.

"Please... I need you to keep—"

"Jimmy. My name is Jimmy."

"Oh...hi, Jimmy. You sound like a brave boy. Are you alone?"

"Yes. No. I mean, I don't know."

Lucy frowned at the reply. What exactly did that mean? Was Jimmy surrounded by floating bodies, not unlike the drowned little girl Lucy had felt and then seen in the horrors of her imagination? Was Jimmy at the epicenter of an orphan graveyard?

She would soon find out. Jimmy's voice was right next to her, muffled slightly by a closed door, which Lucy's hands now felt. Her fingers circled around the coarse texture of the wood, feeling tiny smooth oval and rectangular patches. Lucy guessed them to be stickers. She imagined animated pictures of Superman, Batman, and the Green Lantern. Maybe even Wonder Woman or Cinderella for the little girls.

"Is this the room?" Lucy asked, knocking on the door.

There was a long pause, then Jimmy replied, "Yes."

Lucy found the submerged handle, but it wouldn't turn. "Is the door locked, Jimmy? I cannot open it."

"I'm sorry. Fuzzy and I got scared. We saw the water. Please don't tell Miss Johnson. She'll be really upset at me."

"I'm not telling anybody, Jimmy. Don't worry. Can you get to the door and unlock it for me? Are you close to it?" Lucy was hoping her luck would change; that he'd say yes.

"It's too far," Jimmy said. "I can't swim. Please don't leave us. Please, please. We don't want to die. Don't go."

"I'm not leaving you, Jimmy," Lucy said gently. "I'm going to get us all out of here safely. Just stay calm, okay? Can you do that for me, Jimmy?"

"Okay," Jimmy sniveled, his voice betraying his lack of confidence.

The door and its small handle felt dated, as if they were relics from the 1920s...part of the original house. Lucy felt she wouldn't have to put much weight against the door for it to give way.

But when she pushed against it, she found it was stronger than she'd anticipated. The water only made matters worse; running into it at full speed was not an option when she was barely keeping her head high enough to breathe. She tried punching and kicking, but that worked out exactly as she anticipated.

A last idea popped in her head. The hallway was narrow enough between the walls for her to reach one side with her feet and the other with her hands. If her feet were on the door, she could extend herself with all her strength and press against it until it broke open. Unfortunately, the maneuver would require her to be underwater to do it effectively. Lucy didn't like the thought of having to hold her breath in the nasty deluge, but it was her only option if she planned on keeping her promise to Jimmy.

"I'm going to try something. Just hold on."

Jimmy didn't reply. Lucy prayed she wasn't already too late.

She turned around, dunked her head underwater, and pushed with her legs until her hands felt the wall on the other side. The hallway was about five feet in diameter—just short enough to test her approach. Had it been a foot wider, she would have had to resort to a different strategy.

She pushed with every ounce of energy in her veins, feeling extreme pressure on her wrists and back. The door seemed to budge about a quarter of an inch under her shoes, though it was hard to tell for sure.

She returned the surface, winded.

"What's wrong?" Jimmy asked.

Lucy spit out what had slipped into her mouth during the effort, and waited for a half minute before answering.

"Nothing, Jimmy. We'll get this."

She inhaled a big breath, and repeated the process. This time she pressed until she felt that either her wrists or back would snap in half (perhaps both at the same time, if her luck kept up). She also employed a new tactic: keeping one foot flat on the door, and kicking like hell with the other. This worked much better than just applying flat pressure. She swore she felt the wood crack, and her ears picked up a muffled snap.

Her head shot up, desperately needing air again. She thought Jimmy might again ask her what was wrong, but he remained silent. She hoped he wouldn't get a spark of boldness and try unlocking the door himself.

"One more time," Lucy whispered to herself before filling her lungs with as much air as possible.

She pressed and kicked as if Jimmy were drowning at that moment. She ignored the flood of pain signals that raced to her brain, screaming for her to stop (most of them from her back). She felt and heard another crack, then another.

Lucy felt the tension suddenly vanish as her feet thrust forward, causing her hands to slip from the wall. She returned to the surface, coughed for a spell, then saw the most beautiful sight in front of her.

CHAPTER 11

Light! Glorious light!

Afternoon rays shone through partially drawn blinds, bouncing off the water and painting a wavy reflection on drab white walls and discolored ceiling tiles. It was so bright that Lucy had to cover her eyes for a moment to let her vision adjust.

During this time Jimmy kept repeating that she'd broken the door and that Miss Johnson would be very upset with them.

"My goodness, Jimmy!" Lucy said, staring up at a child sitting in a metal chair, his disheveled brown hair brushing the ceiling and falling in clumps around his frightened, dirty face. The chair was atop a dresser in the corner of the bedroom. Clutched in Jimmy's hands, pulled close to his chest, was a guinea pig stuffed animal.

"Fuzzy said it was the only way," Jimmy said, looking down at his stuffed animal. "We had to play the block game. This time with boxes. One on top of the other to get out of the water."

"You stacked boxes to get up there?" Lucy asked, noting that he was alone in the room. Fuzzy was the person Jimmy had been talking about. "You are both brave and smart, Jimmy. You did exactly what you needed to do."

"Where is Miss Johnson?" Jimmy asked. "And my friends?"

Lucy's mind returned to the drowned little girl in the hallway. She wondered how many others had met a similar fate. "I don't know, Jimmy. Safely away from here, I hope. All I know now is that we have to get you out of this house before the flooding gets worse."

"Can Fuzzy come with us?"

"Yes, sweetie, we're not leaving Fuzzy behind. You just hold on to him tightly as we work our way out of this mess."

Lucy was more than thankful that she could now see what was in front of her. She pushed aside the papers, toys, and an odd assortment of trash that floated in the water, and carefully put one foot in front of the other to avoid tripping on submerged furniture. Spraining her ankle (or receiving a nasty cut on her foot or leg) would spell disaster for both herself and Jimmy.

"How old are you, sweetie?"

Jimmy held out six fingers. It was then that Lucy saw the bluest eyes she had ever seen in her life. How she had not noticed them before astonished her, because they seemed to shine in Jimmy's face, like two tiny windows to a perfectly clear sky. They contrasted brilliantly against the grime on his nose and cheeks.

Jewels, Lucy thought to herself. *Radiant little topaz jewels.*

"A big six years old. When do you turn the big number seven?"

"May 27," Jimmy replied without hesitation. "Fuzzy has the same birthday."

About three feet from the dresser, Lucy's legs hit a solid object. She reached down and felt its straight edges and corners—it was one of the boxes Jimmy had stacked. Their combined height was around four feet, and yet they were completely hidden in the water. Jimmy had been very wise to realize that only the dresser would save his life.

Lucy tried to see if the boxes would help her get closer to Jimmy, but they were now soaked and flimsy, and folded under the pressure of any weight. She easily moved them out of her way.

"I'm not going to be able to stand on anything to reach you, Jimmy. You'll need to jump down into my arms."

Jimmy stared at her with his frightened jewel-like eyes, shaking his head. "We're scared. Fuzzy and I don't want to be in the water."

"It'll be okay, sweetie. We have to get out of here as fast as we can. It isn't safe staying any longer."

Lucy raised her hands out of the water, but Jimmy still shook his head.

"You know when my birthday is, Jimmy?"

"No."

"Today. I was born on this day in California twenty-four years ago."

Jimmy's eyes lit up as if Lucy had told him it was Christmas. "You mean you get cake and presents? Candy, too?"

"Maybe, Jimmy. I don't know until I see my friends again. If I get some, you can be sure I'll share it with everyone who's there." Lucy gave Jimmy a wide smile. "Including a new friend I met today."

"I love chocolate cake. And chocolate ice cream."

"Same with me. I can taste it now! I really want to get out of this house just knowing that, don't you?"

Jimmy nodded happily.

Lucy outstretched her arms again. Jimmy slowly stood up, bending his back to avoid hitting his head on the ceiling. With Fuzzy firmly pressed against his chest, he closed his eyes and dropped from the dresser, landing right in Lucy's embrace with a splash.

Lucy felt a surge of pain in her back again. She had tweaked it opening the door.

"It's warm," Jimmy said, holding Lucy tightly.

"It is. Like a bath. I'm going to move you around so that you are behind me. You know how to ride piggyback, right?"

"But I'll still be in the water."

"Not all the way. You just have to hold on nice and good. I want you to do that for me."

"Okay."

Lucy positioned him correctly, then gradually made her way back out of the bedroom. She first thought opening the window might provide a better escape, but the design of the window pane made it clear she'd have to shatter it to properly exit. The thought of countless shards of broken glass hidden in the water—and in the window frame—didn't sit well in her mind.

"Fuzzy can hold his breath," Jimmy said in Lucy's ear, crouching down. She could feel his warm breath on her skin. "He's like a fish."

"But no gills, right?" Lucy asked, stepping back into the hallway.

She glanced at the direction from which she had come, seeing a long flooded corridor that seemed to stretch forever—becoming pitch black at the end. Returning that same route would mean walking blind again (not to mention passing a dead body). For Jimmy's sake, and for the chance—albeit a slim one—of finding more children alive, she decided the opposite path made more sense.

She waded forward with Jimmy still crouched down, his cheek pressed flat against the top of her head. The light from the bedroom started off strong, revealing more floating papers and trash, but steadily dimmed as Lucy worked her way toward what she hoped was an exit door at the hallway's end. Being on the second floor meant she had to find a fire escape to get out. Any stairs would be useless in the flood, of course. The point was to put herself outside and in a better position to find Adam and get back on the dinghy.

Please be there when we need you, Adam. Please don't leave us waiting in this.

Their original plan had gone to hell. Lucy was supposed to go inside the orphanage with William Lowe and Crissy Walters—the two team members who had been aboard with her on the dinghy—while Adam waited for them outside. Rescue Ravens had a long-standing policy that all missions were group efforts, and that under no circumstance was a member to attempt an objective alone. Director Jamie Price had reiterated this policy before Lucy and her team had gotten aboard the transport helicopter.

But everything had become chaotic as soon as they landed in the Garden District and joined Adam, who had been waiting for them with the boat. A house within the residential community had caught on fire. Firefighters had their hands tied all around the flooded city, so the house was destined to burn until it reached the water—all while filling the air with poisonous smoke. Adam had trouble navigating the dinghy around it. Two times he had to reverse his course and take shortcuts through backyards that had turned into swamps, an eerie sight Lucy would not forget for the rest of her life. It was a war zone. It was identical to the old stories Lucy had read about New Orleans during Hurricane Katrina, a sad reminder that history—though many generations removed—had indeed repeated itself. Only this time there would be no rebuilding of the Big Easy. This time the destruction would be permanent, as was the case with hundreds of other coastal cities around the globe.

Three street blocks before the orphanage, a mother carrying a newborn baby had called for help while standing on the ceiling of a drowned house. The woman looked dehydrated and in terrible shape. Lucy and her team made a hasty decision to break protocol and split up: William and Crissy rescuing the mother and child, Lucy and Adam handling the orphanage. They naively assumed that dividing their team would make them more efficient, able to tackle two jobs in the same amount of time. It was an unwise choice. It took much longer than Adam anticipated to reach the target site due to downed power lines, and once they finally arrived at the orphanage Adam made the gut decision to immediately return to William and Crissy so he could bring them back and reunite the team—thus handling the orphanage together as they had initially planned.

Lucy had reluctantly agreed with his decision. Now, with Jimmy's weight pressing down on her injured back like a backpack filled with stones, she wished she'd never agreed with Adam. She was doing exactly what the Rescue Ravens prohibited. If she ended up dead, and led Jimmy to the same tragic fate, it wouldn't matter what circumstances had snowballed to create their predicament. All that would be remembered was the outcome. She'd end up as a textbook example of a rogue member who had endangered her life along with the life of the child she was trying to save—her impatience and incompetence killing them both.

Lucy shook the dreaded thought away, determined like hell to get Jimmy to safety. She passed another bedroom door. This one was on the opposite side of the hallway from Jimmy's bedroom, and it was open. It was as black as a bottomless pit.

"Hello? Is there anybody in here?"

Lucy waited for a moment while Jimmy shifted his weight so he wouldn't slip off.

"That's for girls only," Jimmy whispered. He added, "They never let me play with their toys."

"Do you know how many were in this room?"

Jimmy thought for a second. "Three. I think."

Lucy thought about the corpse in the water again, its tangled hair floating in darkness around the skull, as still and lifeless as the submerged chair she'd touched right after finding the body.

"I don't hear anyone, do you?"

"Nope," Jimmy answered. "You looking for more to piggyback?"

Lucy chuckled at the question. It felt good to laugh a little. It seemed like years since she'd last done so. "No, sweetie. My spine can only take so much. I'm just trying to see who else needs help, in case we need to return to get them."

"You mean with your friends? The ones with cake and presents?"

"That's right. I have a feeling you're not going to forget that easily."

Lucy waded past the dark bedroom and headed for the closed door at end of the hallway. She heard the thumping of a helicopter change from a distant beat to a loud pounding, and then back to a soft beat again. She hoped she'd heard the noise from behind the door rather than through the ceiling, but either one was equally plausible.

"Do you know where this takes us, Jimmy? Did more kids lock themselves in like you?"

"That's Miss Johnson's. We don't go in there. She gets real mad if we do."

"Does she keep it locked at all times, sweetie? Have you ever tried opening it?"

"Huh-uh. Fuzzy says ghosts are in there. Monsters, too."

Lucy reached the door after some effort and tried the handle. It turned with ease, a welcome change in her luck, and the door cracked open a few inches.

"We won't find ghosts or monsters when we go in. Okay, Jimmy? Cross my heart on it."

"But we'll get in trouble. Miss Johnson will say—"

"Absolutely nothing. We get a free pass today to do what we want. It's like buying a ticket to a theme park and being able to go on all the rides you want, as many times as you want. Nobody is going to say anything to us for what we do."

"You real sure?" Jimmy whispered in her ear.

Lucy could imagine his bright blue eyes staring ahead with apprehension. She pictured him shutting them when they moved forward, avoiding the ghastly sight he had already conjured in his mind.

"If I'm wrong, you get more of my birthday cake. Deal?"

Jimmy waited a short moment. He then put his cheek back on top of her head and softly said, "Okay."

Lucy pushed the door open—not an easy job in five feet of water.

Light stung her eyes, though it wasn't as bad as when she'd entered Jimmy's room (her pupils weren't nearly as dilated as before). A diffused afternoon radiance poured through a mostly immersed glass door, revealing the largest bedroom in the house. It was three times the size of Jimmy's room. The furniture was entirely submerged save for the tops of the bedposts and the last few inches of the headboard—wood buoys resisting the fate of the house. A ceiling fan hung from the center of the room. The fan had a long brass pull chain that dangled all the way into the water. Lucy thought it resembled a fishing line, and imagined some creature taking the bait and turning the fan on in the process.

So weird. So tragic.

"Hey, no monsters or ghosts!" Jimmy said with delight. "They're gone!"

"They never were in here, sweetie. And no people, it seems. The water must have pushed the door closed."

"Can I have that ball?"

"Huh?"

Jimmy pointed so she could see his finger. A small orange ball with a jack-o'-lantern design floated beside one of the protruding bedposts. It was barely bigger than an orange.

Lucy moved to it. Jimmy leaned down, grabbed it, then wobbled as he straightened himself back on Lucy's shoulders.

"Be careful. No ball or toy is worth your life."

"Fuzzy saw it first. He likes it."

"Fuzzy has a good eye. And I spy a possible exit." Lucy fixed her gaze on the large sliding glass door in front of them. It had opened onto a balcony at one point. Three-quarters of it was now hidden from view, beyond which the flood stretched into an endless river in the street.

"But more water will come in if we open it," Jimmy said with fear. "It will get us. We won't be able to breathe."

"It's the same level outside as it is inside, sweetie. We don't have to worry about it going over our heads." *But if another levee fails...or if we accidently step off the balcony because of a missing railing...* Lucy kept her thoughts to herself, not wanting to frighten Jimmy.

She waded to the glass door. She heard the thumping of another helicopter, but this one kept its distance and was gone within seconds. She reached down, felt blindly around the door with both hands, and after some effort found the handle.

She pulled on it.

Nothing.

She pulled again—same result.

"Damn you," Lucy hissed at it.

"That's a bad word," Jimmy said. "Miss Johnson will wash your mouth out for it."

"As she should. This thing won't open."

She felt the sliding lock on the door handle and tried flipping it up and down while pulling at each stop. It wouldn't budge. Lucy said, "There must be a bar at the bottom blocking it."

"Candy bar?"

Lucy laughed. "That would be one really huge candy bar, don't you think?"

Jimmy laughed with her. Hearing his laughter made Lucy's heart glow.

He should be laughing all the time, not going through this nightmare. He's barely six... This was another thought she would keep to herself.

"I meant a sliding door bar lock, sweetie. A metal bar. They sometime use them with these kinds of doors so bad people cannot break into the house. Have you ever held your breath before?"

"Lots! I used to play a game with Lucas. He was my best friend before he had to go away. We pretended the hallway was a tunnel, and we had to stop breathing as we ran all the way down it."

"Did you make it the whole way?"

"Twice. Almost three times, but Lucas said I cheated and I couldn't count the last one."

"I need you do it again. Only this time, it's going to be underwater. You just do the same thing you did in that game and hold on to my head as I go under. If you need to grab my hair so you don't fall, that's fine too."

"But what if I need air? What if I can't hold it anymore?"

"Then you just tap on my ear and I'll know we need to go back to the surface. I promise we won't be under long. I'll make it fast."

Jimmy stayed silent for a moment. Lucy was surprised when he responded, "Got it."

"Great! You're a brave boy, Jimmy. Like I said, it'll be fast. I will count to three, okay?"

"Yup."

"Here we go. One... Two... Three..."

CHAPTER 12

Lucy bent her knees and waist, quickly sinking into the water. Jimmy had his palms firmly pressed on either side of her head—his hands at the ready in case he panicked and needed to tap on her ears. Lucy went straight to the bottom of the door frame. She moved with urgency, working blind yet again, relying on her fingers to feel out the object in question. At first all she found was the aluminum frame and the rubber texture of the adhesive sealant keeping the door in place. But then she detected a thin length of metal. It was square and felt very similar to the frame itself. Just as Jimmy tapped her ears, she grabbed it and shot to the surface—thankful it didn't stick in the frame.

Lucy and Jimmy heaved for air.

"Got that little sneaker," Lucy said at length, wiping water from her eyes.

"Sorry we couldn't go longer," Jimmy said. "Fuzzy and I got scared."

"You two were great. You did exactly as you needed to do, and now we should be able to get the heck out of this place."

Lucy pulled on the handle. The door slid open, albeit slowly. She got it open just wide enough to squeeze through without bruising herself or Jimmy. She was careful not to move hastily, still fearful of a missing balcony railing (or even part of the balcony itself). Stepping off the second floor wouldn't prove disastrous if she had been alone—all she'd have to do was swim back—but it was an entirely different situation with Jimmy on her shoulders. She couldn't stay afloat while carrying him.

Now on the edge of the balcony, feeling the hidden safety railing against her hip and legs, Lucy stared out at historic St. Charles Avenue with an eerie feeling of déjà vu, thinking that the sight in front of her was the same one she'd seen when glancing out of the transport helicopter as they made their landing approach in New Orleans. What she had seen then was the Mississippi River. It had been wide and bloated. The water stretched north and south beyond her ability to see its beginning or end, and it had seemed to stand still, as if it were made of rippled glass.

St. Charles Avenue was now that river. The road and streetcar tracks were well-covered, along with the cars parked at the curb. Houses, trees, power lines—everything was half-covered with water, making the Garden District a flooded hellhole for the unfortunate residents who hadn't managed to escape nature's wrath.

Lucy fished out her waterproof radio transceiver from her pocket and pressed the outgoing message trigger. "Adam, it's Lucy. Do you hear me? Are you there, Adam?"

"What's that?" Jimmy asked, bending down from Lucy's shoulders to get a better look. He stared intently with his radiant blue eyes.

"It's a device that lets me talk with my friends. It's old technology, but it's all that really works in conditions like this."

"Can I play too?"

"I'm afraid it's not a toy, sweetie. If we drop it by accident or break it somehow, our chances of finding my friends will be very slim."

"Will they bring cake when they come? I'm really hungry."

"I bet you are. We will get you some food soon, Jimmy. I promise."

Lucy pressed on the transceiver again. "Adam, come in. It's Lucy. I've rescued a child at the orphanage and we are now standing on a second floor balcony on the western end. We need you to get us."

She let go of the trigger; static filled the speaker. She glanced at the far edges of St. Charles Avenue, hoping to see a dinghy appear from one of the intersecting streets, but all was still.

"Adam, come in. Adam…" Lucy blankly stared down at the transceiver and shook her head.

"Damn it, Adam," she said softly under her breath. Jimmy's constant weight on her shoulders was making the pain in her back worse. She desperately wanted to put him down, but the flood was too high for his height, and holding him afloat wasn't a better option.

"They aren't coming, are they?"

"Yes they are. I'm sorry, sweetie. I shouldn't have said that bad word. I'm just frustrated, that's all. They will come if it takes me standing here all day and night to keep calling them."

At length Jimmy said, "Fuzzy wants to know where all the water came from. Was it a bad storm?"

"No, but that's a good guess. This was something different. It came from the ocean. Does Fuzzy know what a levee is?"

Jimmy put the stuffed animal in front of Lucy's face and shook its head side to side.

"It's a wall that protects a city from flooding. There are many of these walls around where you live because all these houses are lower than the water. That means the water is always trying to get in, but the levees stop that from happening. They block the path."

"Someone took them away? A monster?"

"No one did anything like that. This didn't happen because of a person stealing. No monsters, either."

"But you said it wasn't a storm? Fuzzy is confused."

"It's a bit hard to explain, Jimmy, but the short answer is that the water kept getting higher and higher every year. It got to the point where those walls couldn't hold it all anymore and broke. Have you ever seen dominos fall before?"

Jimmy nodded yes with his stuffed animal.

"It was like that. One levee fell, and then more followed in other places that were weak. That's why you see all of this now. This is all water that used to be in the ocean."

"Fuzzy says they should put it back. So do I. We don't like it."

"That makes three of us. I wish we could take all this mess away." Lucy tried the transceiver again. "Adam, are you there? This is Lucy. Please come in. Adam, it's Lucy. Hello?"

She and Jimmy listened to the soft hum of static for several minutes. A chill worked down Lucy's spine as she noticed that the neighborhood was completely silent save the noise from her speaker. It was as if the flood had not only drowned the cars and houses, but the voices of the people who had once walked the sidewalks, boarded the streetcars, laughed in the playgrounds. She found herself wondering how many other people had met the same end as the little girl she'd discovered in the orphanage. How many of them had been trapped and killed and silenced?

"I'm cold," Jimmy said, shivering as he said it.

Lucy reached up and rubbed his arms as best she could. A fresh surge of pain exploded in her back. She bit her lip to fight back the urge to cry out— biting too hard, as it turned out; she tasted the coppery flavor of fresh blood on her tongue.

The silence of the transceiver only made her pain worse. Lucy had to keep talking to distract herself. "Jimmy, do you remember which state I told you I was from?"

He thought for a moment. "California. Me and Fuzzy have a puzzle map. It's a big piece on it. Not as big as Alaska."

"Very smart, boy. You're a good listener. Well, when I was your age the problem in my state was just the opposite of this one. We had too little water. There were really long and bad droughts. They lasted for years and years, and sometimes we'd turn the faucet on and nothing would come out. We would go weeks just drinking from emergency bottles my grandma had stocked up in a supply shed. I remember one hot summer seeing only a half-gallon of water left in that shed. All the other bottles around it were bone dry. That single bottle was the only thing we had for me, my grandma, and my uncle."

"Your mom and dad, too?"

"I never knew my parents. They both died when I was very young."

"You were an orphan like me and Fuzzy!"

"Hey, you're right. Funny...I never thought about that all this time with you. It seems like we have something in common." A thin smile stretched across Lucy's face.

"Fuzzy doesn't like being an orphan. Me either. We wish we were like other kids."

"What happened to your mom and dad, Jimmy?"

"They are angels now. That's what Miss Johnson told me. She said they went to heaven after a car crash. Do you believe in angels?"

"I think it's very possible one led me on the path to rescue you. But we can never know for sure about that sort of thing, can we? It's always a mystery."

"Someday I'm going to find one and not let it fly away. Fuzzy is going to help me. We are going to keep it forever."

"That's a big plan, sweetie," Lucy replied, laughing. "When that happens, you let me know, okay?"

"Okay. I promise. Lucy...are you going to stay with me and Fuzzy?"

The question caught Lucy by surprise. Before she could give an answer, Adam's distant voice cut through the silence.

"Lucy! Lucy!"

Her eyes shot in his direction, seeing a crowded dinghy work its way toward her. Adam was standing and waving wildly. William and Crissy were seated in front of him, along with the mother and baby they had rescued.

"They're here!" Jimmy shouted.

Lucy's heart jumped out of her chest with relief and joy. She quickly grabbed the transceiver and spoke into it. "Adam! God am I glad to see you!"

More static spit out of the transceiver; she frowned at it.

"Lucy, my battery is dead!" Adam yelled from the boat, now waving his transceiver at her. "Just hold tight! Be right there!"

It took only a few minutes for the dinghy to reach them. Jimmy boarded first—Crissy took the boy in her arms and safely sat him beside the mother and baby. William then assisted Lucy, reaching out with his long limbs and pulling her as best he could without falling in the water himself.

"Ouch!" Lucy said, cringing from a jolt of pain in her back. "Careful."

"Sorry," William replied with a look of confusion, pulling her with more delicacy. "Are you okay?"

Lucy successfully stepped into the dinghy and felt her exhausted legs give out as she plopped down beside Jimmy. The suddenness at which she'd taken a seat surprised even herself.

"I am now," Lucy said, briefly feeling her back, then putting an arm over Jimmy's shoulders.

Adam gave Lucy a surprise kiss on her mouth. "I cannot tell you how happy I am to see that you are okay, Lucy! You won't believe why it took us so long to get here."

"Save that story for later on. All I want right now is to get back to dry land, please."

Adam nodded and turned back to the motor.

Not a word was spoken as the dinghy made its way down the river that was now St. Charles Avenue. An endless line of ruined Victorian houses—many of which were centuries old—slipped by one after another, like elaborate sarcophagi from a vanished society, the remnants of a global civilization in disarray.

None of it seemed real to Lucy. At one point she turned her attention to the newborn baby nestled in the mother's arms, and she saw the infant's deep brown eyes stare straight back at her. The baby didn't smile. It simply stared with an intense, soul-penetrating curiosity, absorbing the world into which it had been born.

Lucy held her gaze on the searching, hungry eyes.

Welcome, little one.

PART III
AIR

CHAPTER 13

The answer to Jimmy's question was yes. Lucy never left the boy's side, adopting him when he was eight (after a nightmare of paperwork and bureaucratic hassles). She married Adam the same year the adoption became official, and they moved their little family to Bangor, Maine—a location, Lucy was sure, that made her dear Uncle Neil roll over in his grave.

The decision to move far northeast was simple: it was one of the few places in the United States that wasn't being decimated by climate change. No droughts. No floods, if you lived at least thirty minutes inland. The summer months were incredible, and the long cold winters that used to hammer the region had become mild and virtually indistinguishable from the warmer seasons. In a sense, Maine—and several neighboring states—had become the new Florida, experiencing an unprecedented population explosion in what the press labeled GWM (Global Warming Migration).

Lucy's childhood friend Rachel had also played a part in the decision. Rachel had reconnected with her after reading an article about the Rescue Ravens that included Lucy's name and picture.

"You've got a family to look after now, Lucy," Rachel had said over the phone. "My parents' choice to move to Augusta was the best thing that ever happened to us. Trust me on this. You won't regret it at all. Maine is a no-brainer."

While the reasons to move were very clear, the choice itself had been a difficult one for Lucy. She'd thought about the people who couldn't relocate because of money, health, or work-related issues. It wasn't fair that they should be left behind to struggle and fight in the chaos they hadn't created. Following the path of the GWM seemed morally wrong—a form of selling out on her long-standing principles.

Eventually a medical examination had tipped the scales in favor of leaving. Lucy and Adam had watched a radiologist pull up an MRI scan of Lucy's back and circle the herniated disc that was causing her so much pain. He'd stated that while surgery might not be needed, she would certainly have to avoid all strenuous activities that would likely cause further damage.

Lucy had immediately understood the underlying message: her field days with the Rescue Ravens were over.

Three months after her diagnosis, Lucy and her family had packed up and driven to Bangor. The population was hovering near two million residents at the time. It had been an astronomical growth explosion for the city since the days when Stephen King had called it home—the population was about sixty times the recorded United States census estimate the year of the prolific author's death. The city's supporting infrastructure mirrored the complexity of Los Angeles. A half-dozen highways stitched around and through the city, pushing the boundaries at the edges while swallowing the commercial and residential districts in the center. The open fields and lots of generations past had long since vanished, succumbing to the inevitable forces of development and commercialism.

The changes weren't just isolated to Bangor. Sanford, Augusta, Lincoln— just about every non-coastal town up and down New England had been transformed in much the same way by the constant flood of Americans seeking a solution to their vanishing dreams. Home was no longer home. The heart of the land of the free was quickly becoming too costly and dangerous for the average family to bear, and all that could be done was follow the road of least resistance—where a more forgiving sun shone from a merciful sky.

Lucy, Adam, and Jimmy had found that sanctuary in Maine. For a decade, Bangor had exceeded their most fanciful expectations of the city, providing a bubble of perfect weather, stable employment, and steady growth. They lived in a modest two-story house near the Walden-Parke Preserve, a comfortable five miles northeast of downtown. Their neighborhood was relatively safe and quiet. The only crime to hit their area during that ten-year stretch had been a burglary two houses down, which came a few months before their seven-year anniversary. Nothing of significant value had been stolen.

Adam had taken a job as a boat mechanic at Pushaw Lake, working tirelessly year-round as an independent contractor. Lucy had found employment in budgeting and planning for the administrative department at Martin Luther High, the school Jimmy would be graduating from in the next four months. It was a family joke that Lucy only worked at the school to keep an eye on her son. Whenever Jimmy's friends echoed this thought in jest, Jimmy would quickly retort that it was *he* who needed to look after his adventurous mother...not the other way around.

Something in the water seemed to keep Adam and Lucy looking youthful and healthy through the years. If it weren't for a few grey hairs sneaking out on Lucy's head, and a patch of missing hairs on Adam's, one could reasonably deduce they'd stumbled upon the antidote to the slow venom of aging. Their faces and fit physiques had remained untouched by the many spent seasons. This was in stark contrast to their neighbors, who were hit hard with every sunrise and moonset, wrinkling like dried fruit, bloating like rising bread.

But Lucy and Adam only needed to look within their own house for a juxtaposition of how a decade could age a person. A height chart tacked to a bedroom wall had date marks at four feet, four feet and four inches, four feet and seven inches, and five feet—where the chart stopped. A shelf on a hallway closet displayed three pairs of sneakers side-by-side: a size 13 (boy's child), a size 6 (boy's youth), and a size 9 (men's adult). A sequence of large family pictures hanging in the living room showed the remarkable transformation of an adorable blue-eyed child radiating with youth's innocence into a gorgeous tall and dark young man, his eyes retaining every millimeter of their jewel-like quality.

It was impossible for Lucy and Adam to ignore the passage of time; Jimmy was their constant reminder.

The boy's physical growth was matched by his emotional and mental development. Jimmy was mature and humble beyond his years, due in large part to his experiences at the orphanage. His grades were consistently at the top of his class. His peers had elected him as senior class president—a status that, when combined with his exceptional looks, made him the most sought-after date among the girls going to prom.

"He's so calm and collected about it all," Lucy told Adam a day before Jimmy's 18th birthday. "I cannot imagine being his age and having so much on my mind. I'd go crazy in a few minutes."

"You?" Adam asked with a raised eyebrow, standing beside Lucy in the kitchen as they worked on Jimmy's birthday cake together. "Miss Supergirl? Miss *I'll storm the castle alone and bring out the survivors on my back?*"

"That's different. I had some training, and it was many years after high school. I was older than him."

"Maybe you're too close to Jimmy to see it, but he gets it from you. Your strength has rubbed off on the boy. I sure as heck know it didn't come from me."

"You don't think his biological parents factor in it at all?" Lucy asked, spelling out Jimmy's name with green frosting. "I read an article the other day that said genes can play a much larger role than upbringing in shaping an adopted kid's life. It gave examples of parents who were at their wit's end trying to turn problem children around. Maybe it has nothing to do with us. Maybe we just got lucky with Jimmy."

"We did get lucky. But that was with finding him. That was with getting him out before he drowned in that damn awful hell that killed New Orleans. The good fortune we've experienced ever since leaving occurred because we took active measures to work hard and raise him in a proper environment. Pardon my crudeness, but that article is full of shit if they think it applies to all families. You cannot paint in broad strokes like that. Every household is different."

Lucy smiled and nodded. But secretly she still had her doubts. The column she had read made her question her influence on Jimmy's life, downplaying her one heroic moment as just a fluke of the past, and minimizing the impact of any parental lessons she had given to him to date. She felt small and inconsequential.

Lucy continued to harbor that insecure feeling for another full month following Jimmy's birthday. She kept it to herself, never bothering to bring it up again with Adam or any of her coworkers or friends. She considered buying books on the matter to see what conclusions the authors reached—to see if they supported what she'd read, or debunked it—but she soon found all the proof she would ever need while on a school field trip.

Martin Luther High had a Big Buddy-Little Buddy program with Bangor Elementary School (BES), in which seniors would pair up with first and second graders a few days out of the year to take educational field trips together. The two schools were only three miles apart, and the goal was to give younger kids role models in the community with whom they could talk, play, and shadow. Jimmy had been a little buddy himself while at BES. He vividly remembered the experience, the trips to the zoo and children's museum, recalling with great fondness how an older kid named Mark Haslett had made him feel welcome and safe in a strange new city.

Jimmy had immediately signed up for the program the first day of his senior year. His little buddy was a six-year-old first grader named Randy Preston, an African American boy with a wide smile and a fascination for sleight of hand card tricks. Randy was born in Bangor; his parents had moved there from Atlanta, Georgia when the reservoir wars in the city became too hostile and exhausting. Jimmy and Randy had been on two field trips together: one to Bangor Waterfront and the other to the Gracie Theatre at Husson University.

The third trip, scheduled to be their last, was to the Bangor City Forest to see the maple and birch trees, wild calla, and cinnamon fern. The vegetation had remained largely intact in the warmer climate, but the wildlife hadn't been so fortunate, suffering significant reductions and habitat extinctions. Birds, squirrels, and rabbits thrived. The larger animals had faded away into pictures and stats on the forestry history list, leaving indelible, yearning impressions on the minds of the readers as to what they might have really looked like up close and in person.

Three adults were chaperoning the field trip. The one with the most experience was Kim Perry, a second-grade teacher who hadn't missed a single Big Buddy-Little Buddy event in the five years she had been employed at BES. She was in her mid-thirties, and was the natural selection to lead the trip. Bill Newman, forty-six, was second in line in terms of experience. He'd signed on two years after Kim, and enjoyed using the trips to help teach his first-grade students about basic biology and geology. Bill was a born and raised Bangor native who knew a great deal about the city's recreation sites.

The last chaperone was a complete rookie. She was the mother of one of the big buddies on the trip, and volunteered because she wanted to help the kids experience something educational and enlightening beyond the classroom. She used her contacts in the admin department at Martin Luther High to secure a spot normally filled by another teacher. While the work itself wasn't hard—just general supervision of the kids to make sure they were safe and free from trouble—a significant legal liability hovered over both schools if the children were injured because of a chaperone's negligence. This worry was not unfounded: a disgruntled parent had filed a lawsuit during the program's fifth year when her child had broken his arm while running irresponsibly in a museum. The suit had been settled, but the resulting unease had never dissipated.

"I promise to use good judgment, and do whatever Kim and Bill need me to do," Lucy told the school's principal. "You have my word."

Lucy's word was almost unnecessary. An unusual winter jet stream had pushed into New England, bringing cold air and thunderstorms. Local meteorologists predicted that the worst of it would hit several days after the scheduled trip, but there was still a chance for rain and light snow flurries during the beginning part of the week.

Kim and Bill considered canceling. They had come close to announcing their decision, but changed their minds after seeing an updated weather report showing that the jet stream had weakened over Bangor, drastically reducing the likelihood of tempestuous skies on the day of the trip.

Leaving as scheduled, forty two kids piled into a standard electric school bus—eighteen seniors with twenty-four little buddies (a few seniors had two or three buddies). Kim, Bill, and Lucy sat in the front. The ride to the forest was a fairly short one: the forest was just ten minutes north of the schools on I-95. The bus driver was a forty-something man named Gregg whose lean physique reminded Lucy of her late Uncle Neil.

Gregg was good at keeping order on his bus, telling all passengers at the beginning, "Stay seated and silent, or see me rise and get violent."

As was custom, the students sat with their buddies—talking and playing games on the ride over. Jimmy and Randy were three seats behind Lucy. Jimmy had brought a deck of playing cards to show Randy some magic tricks he'd learned from a video he'd seen by a professional.

"Okay, now pick two," Jimmy told Randy after shuffling the deck and fanning the cards out. "It doesn't matter which ones. Just don't let me see them."

Randy displayed his wide smile and reached for one in the middle and one on the end. "Two?" Randy asked. "All tricks I've seen are with just one card."

"Not this trick. You'll see. Now take a good look at the cards you picked and don't forget them."

"Okay. Got it."

"Good. I will turn my head and let you put them back. I promise not to look at them." Jimmy closed his eyes and turned.

Randy did as he was instructed, his smile even wider than before. "Now what?" Randy asked.

"Now I shuffle the deck again, and then let you shuffle them. When we are done, I'll show you your cards."

"Oh man. This I gotta see."

Jimmy laughed. After taking turns mixing the cards, Jimmy set the deck in a nice, even stack.

"I want you to pick out the top card."

Randy narrowed his eyes at Jimmy, disbelieving the trick. He picked it out.

"Well?" Jimmy asked.

"Holy smokes! The queen of hearts! It worked!"

"Only halfway so far. We still have more to do."

"Is the other on the top, too?"

"Nope. This one is here."

From the very bottom of the deck, Jimmy pulled out the card: four of clubs.

"No way! That's crazy!"

Randy's eyes were as wide as saucers. Jimmy threw his head back and laughed, taking the cards back.

The sound of his laughter reached Lucy. She turned and saw her son showing Randy the cards he had picked out. A thin smile creased her face watching them. She recalled the first poker game she had seen as a kid, in a distant time that seemed more like a dream now than a memory. She still remembered the delicious, stringy quesadilla Helen Day had made, the strong odor of the cigar smoke hovering in the room, the look of surprise and rage in Pat Day's face as her uncle revealed the winning hand of the night. Her smile faded as she thought about Grandma Clara's passing (heart failure) when Lucy was Jimmy's current age, and then her Uncle Neil's death (lung cancer) when she was twenty-two. She wished they'd gotten to see Jimmy and met Adam. She wished she could bring them back so they could all have dinner together as a family—one Lucy would cook for days to make it special. Maybe even little Fuzzy could join in that grand feast of her united family, she thought.

Does Jimmy even remember Fuzzy anymore? Does that little stuffed guinea pig still hold a loving place somewhere deep in my grown son's heart?

"Are you ready to do this?"

Lucy shot back around, the question taking her by surprise. "I'm sorry?" Lucy asked.

"To keep this zoo in order out there," Kim Perry said. Her blonde hair was tied back in a tight ponytail to the point of nearly stretching her forehead. It hurt Lucy just to look at it. "We are far outnumbered, you know. We've got to be generals out there. I hope you're ready for that."

"Generals?" Lucy asked, snickering at the thought. "Does it really get that bad?"

"It can, if we let them get out of control. We can't have more broken bones. It was years ago, but I'm sure you heard about that one. Ted Paxton was in charge back then. That man was the biggest pushover I've ever met. The school was lucky it was just the boy's arm and not his life."

"You're the boss, Kim. Like the old saying goes, you tell me to jump, I ask how high."

Kim displayed a bright set of white teeth at the response. "That's what I want the kids to ask you. But to have fun too, of course. That too."

"Of course," Lucy said, picturing Kim as the exhausting general in her own house: pointing fingers, shouting orders, keeping the zoo that was her family always in check.

The bus turned into a parking lot and pulled to a stop.

"This is our space station!" Gregg shouted, looking in his rearview mirror while opening the door.

Kim shot up. "You heard him, kids! Everyone line up nice and pretty and wait your turn to get out. I don't want to see pushing or shoving." Kim turned to be the front of the line.

Before standing and taking her place, Lucy briefly glanced out her window at a thin line of clouds that were barely visible on the horizon. Goosebumps pricked up all over her body.

The clouds were dark. The darkest she'd ever seen.

CHAPTER 14

The Orono Bog Boardwalk was a one-mile trail loop on the northeastern edge of the Bangor City Forest. The boards cut through bog maples, cinnamon ferns, and skunk cabbage; eventually circling peat moss and carnivorous pitcher plants at the bog's center. An adjoining trail had recently been added that extended the hike another two miles into the forest, which fed into a wide campground filled with picnic tables and restrooms.

The students had been told weeks in advance to pack sack lunches so they could eat outside when they reached the end of the trail. The majority of students remembered the instruction. A few had forgotten, as was expected, but they would be able to rely on the handful of extra lunches Lucy had stored in her backpack (along with extra water, four blankets, and a first-aid kit). Lucy had beaten Kim and Bill to the punch during their first pre-trip meeting: she'd volunteered to bring the provisions before they even asked her to do so. Bill had told Lucy he was highly impressed. Lucy had replied that anyone in her shoes would be thinking the same when dealing with kids.

The group reached the picnic tables at a quarter till noon. They'd seen plenty of plants along the way, but they hadn't had much luck with the park's animals. They'd only spotted two red-winged blackbirds, a squirrel, and rabbit that looked like a snowshoe hare (the rabbit had been a good distance away, so it was impossible to determine with certainty). The younger boys were disappointed they hadn't seen any garter snakes or northern leopard frogs, while the younger girls had their hearts set on white-tailed deer and barred owls (both of which were still in the forest).

Nevertheless, spirits were high while everyone ate their lunches. The surrounding maple and birch trees provided an enriching beauty and serenity that just couldn't be duplicated in the classroom. The air smelled fresh. The sound of the wind threading through the forest had a soft harmony to it—as if the trees were whispering the lyrics of a song long forgotten, a song that accompanied a dance once held sacred to the people of the land.

Lucy was seated next to Jimmy and Randy at a picnic table along with four other students. She closed her eyes about halfway into her lunch and let the cool breeze cleanse her face. She felt absolutely relaxed in that moment. Her mind was focused on appreciation rather than meditation, on being grateful for being outdoors and experiencing nature's spiritual enlightenment.

Her thoughts fluttered like butterflies in that tranquil state for a good two minutes.

Upon opening her eyes, her mood was instantly transformed into one of terrifying shock.

"What's wrong, Mom?" Jimmy asked, seeing the fear in Lucy's eyes as she stared at the sky behind him. Jimmy swung around. He immediately saw it too: a sky billowing with clouds that were as dark as they were ominous.

"Lunch is over," Lucy said, throwing the uneaten remains of her meal in her bag. "We must head back to the bus now." She got up and dashed across the campground to the picnic table where Kim was seated with more students. "Kim, it's time to get everyone together. We cannot stick around any longer."

"Why is that?" Kim asked without concern, taking a sip from her water.

"That's reason number one." Lucy pointed to the approaching storm.

Kim's eyes widened with surprise upon seeing it. "Oh, look at that. It's gotten even darker, hasn't it?"

"I'll tell Bill, too. We'll get the kids ready in just a few minutes."

"Well, the older kids wanted to see Buxton Stream...it's only fifteen minutes from here. There's a small trail that leads to it, and it's fairly well marked."

Lucy's brow stitched together. "Kim, we don't have time for another trail. Fifteen minutes can make a big difference in weather like this. It can quickly turn on you. I've seen it happen."

"I've been in storms before, too, Lucy," Kim said with a condescending tone. "I'm very good at gauging their strength and speed. I saw those clouds in the distance a few hours ago, and they've been moving really slowly ever since. They *do* look bad, I'll give you that, but if we move quickly we should be able see that stream and then make it all the way back before it hits us."

"Maybe the older kids. But we can't get the younger ones to move like that. Not for three miles without rest."

"Are you suggesting we break up the group, Lucy?"

"I'm saying we all need to head back now, Kim," Lucy replied, her frustration building. "That storm is just too close for comfort. It could be a nightmare for us, dressed the way we are. All shirts and shorts." Lucy glanced at the clouds again, then turned back to Kim, exhaling a long breath to stay calm. "Look, maybe you are right and I'm completely wrong about the timing on this. I don't want to split the group, but the younger kids need to return so we don't risk it. I can take them. You can go with the big buddies and get pictures and such to share later on. If they really seem bent on going, that is."

Kim held up her hands in surrender. "Have it your way, Lucy. You take half, and I'll get the other. But you know you're going to be hearing about it from the little buddies all the way back. Even after all they've seen."

"I'll be the witch who spoiled their trip. Yes, that's probably right. I guess it's good that I've never really let that sort of thing bother me much."

Lucy opened her mouth to tell Kim one last time that everyone should return immediately, but then sighed and said nothing. She knew she'd be wasting her breath trying to get it all her way; it was clear that Kim would not budge further on the issue. The compromise had been made.

When Lucy told Bill the plan, he replied that he'd help her take the kids back. "I'll be the bad guy too, Lucy. Please don't say anything to Kim, but I'm with you on this one. I think it's completely crazy to hang around. Those so-called weather experts screwed up today's forecast, that's for sure. There's no way we aren't going to see some amount of rain or wind before sunset."

Lucy was surprised when she explained the change of plans to the younger kids. A few of them groaned, but the majority didn't put up a fuss when they saw the reason for her decision: the imminent tempest spoke for itself. Randy was the voice of the majority when he saw it and exclaimed, "Whoa! Look at that! We gotta get the heck out of here!"

"I'm going with you, Mom," Jimmy said, quickly eating the last few bites of his lunch.

"Right by your side," came a female voice at the table. It was Shannon Andrews, a student in Jimmy's class whose deep brown eyes and strong cheekbones could still be seen under the curved bill of her baseball cap. Her quick, fiery wit was well known to all of the seniors. "Randy and the munchkins will get back just fine. It's Jimmy I'm worried about."

She grinned at Jimmy. Jimmy laughed, returning the smile.

"Okay, you two get the kids together, and don't forget to tell them to use the restrooms now if they have to go," Lucy said while unzipping her backpack. She pulled out two of her blankets. "Here, Bill...give these to Kim, no matter what she says. I've got another two in my bag in case we find ourselves in a fix. If she needs extra water, I've got some."

"You got it," Bill replied, taking the blankets and jogging across the campground.

Lucy checked the time: 12:55 pm. She guesstimated they would reach the bus around 2:30 if they made good speed and didn't take any long rest stops. A 2:00 arrival would be wishful thinking, and 3:00 would be a worst-case scenario—one that would spell havoc for Kim and her group, caught in the same conditions.

Lucy felt a tug at her leg; it was Randy, holding Jimmy's playing cards.

"Do you want to see a magic trick I learned today?"

Lucy kneeled down to his level. "Not right now, sweetheart. You can show me later, when we get back to the bus. Do you have to use the restroom?"

Randy shook his head and looked down at his feet. "I'm kinda scared. I want to go home now."

Lucy put a soft hand on his shoulder. "Everything is going to be okay. We will get you home faster than any magic you've ever seen. It will even be better than a card trick."

Randy's head shot up. "Oh, nothing is better than that! I can't wait to show you my new magic."

"Neither can I. But it better be really good, Randy. I'm paying top dollar for the show." She gave Randy a wink.

"We're all ready now, Mom."

Lucy straightened herself, and focused her attention on Jimmy, Bill, Shannon, and the little buddies huddled around them. She was glad to see that if any of the kids shared Randy's fear, they were doing an excellent job of controlling it. It would make their trip back much easier.

"Great, let's get moving," Lucy said to the group. "Remember to stay close together, and make sure to look out for each other. Lead the way, Jimmy."

Jimmy moved to the front and walked with a brisk but manageable pace. The group funneled into a line behind him, with Bill and Shannon bringing up the rear. Lucy decided to be the very last in line to make sure she could keep an eye on any stragglers.

Before she left the campground, she glanced over her shoulder and locked eyes with Kim. Lucy's stomach tightened with a strong feeling of dread at the compromise they had reached. While Kim's face did not betray any sign of regret or remorse at splitting the group, Lucy could sense a growing unease behind her mask of confidence. It hadn't built to the point of changing Kim's mind, but it was definitely swelling.

Part III - Air

Kim turned her back to Lucy without waving. Lucy shook her head, and quickly walked to catch up with her group.

CHAPTER 15

Lucy once read an article that stated the term "global warming" could be better understood if it were labeled "global weirding." The focus of the piece was to show—with decades of collected data—that warmer temperatures around the planet, year after year, typically led to weather conditions that were highly abnormal and unstable. The author layered a Celsius chart atop a graph of all the irregular weather events that had been reported worldwide in that same timeframe. The resulting graphic showed a direct correlation between the two variables. The author admitted that he had expected such a connection, but that the ratio of the percentage link had surprised him: for every one percent increase in Celsius, the frequency of reported abnormal weather observances increased four percent. This parallel relationship existed on six of the seven continents. The article provided a long list of cities that experienced droughts, floods, blizzards, and a wide variety of other weather-related conditions that were either highly unusual in the region, or had lasted far longer than anticipated.

Lucy remembered how the article showed weather weirding as it applied to several New England cities: Boston, Providence, and New Haven. Many generations before Lucy's birth, much of the northeastern United States had been hammered with a mixture of droughts and heat waves during the summer months, and brutal, record-breaking blizzards during the colder seasons. The temperature swings had been unfathomable. Boston broke two records in the same year (45 degrees Celsius in August, and -52 degrees Celsius in January), and the following year both Providence and New Haven posted eight straight days of record highs, the sun baking the towns without remorse at all hours of the day.

Lucy's mind returned to that article once again while jogging with the children as she felt the first pinpricks of hail strike her skin. It started off slow and insignificant: sporadic white pellets no bigger than grape seeds tapping her arms and legs in long intervals, like they were toying with her. Then the storm advanced to pea-sized beads falling in sheets, stinging all parts of her exposed body. Finally the sky proceeded to hail as large as avocado pits, knocking the planks on the boardwalk so hard it sounded like a chorus of drumbeats.

The larger ice was brutal on the group. The children shouted out in pain, and several started to cry either because of the agony, or for fear it would grow worse.

Lucy provided the only solution she could muster for the kids—her two blankets. She, Jimmy, Shannon, and Bill each held a corner as high as they could reach, spreading them out over the huddled group like a protective canopy. It was a tight fit for the children beneath it; they had to squeeze in to ensure complete cover.

"Don't stop!" Lucy shouted at the kids over the hammering of the boards, now taking Jimmy's place in leading the group. "Stay together and just keep walking with us!"

The hail quickly covered the boardwalk in white. Lucy felt her shoes crunch on the lumpy ice as she pushed forward against a strong, bitter wind. The dark sky was now completely choked with menacing clouds; not a sliver of sun penetrated it.

Lucy calculated that they'd covered a little over two miles in the last hour. They had less than a mile left, most of it in open territory with very few trees, but to everyone in the group that distance might as well have been a thousand miles. Their pace had been significantly reduced. Visibility of their path was as poor as their traction upon it. The trail that had been so easy and inconsequential just hours earlier was now an unrecognizable nightmare.

"Keep going!" Lucy shouted under the blankets, seeing some of the children pause. "Stopping will only make it worse. Keep up with the group."

"But I'm cold and tired," a kid yelled back, crying.

"Me too," came the whimper of another.

Lucy nodded in understanding and replied, "I know you are. We will get you warm soon. Do not stop!"

But then the hail became too fierce, forcing even the adults to halt and seek protection under the makeshift shield. Ice roughly the size of golf balls rained down as if the sky had split open and emptied the last remnants of a dying glacier. Lucy was certain the onslaught would break the bones in her hand. Unlike her protected face and body, her fingers were completely exposed to the wrath of the barrage while holding the blankets. The bombardment was akin to getting pelted with rocks. It hurt like hell every time an ice chunk hit her square; she had to fight with all her strength not to let go and nurse her wounds.

"Shit," Lucy whispered to herself, watching with dismay as hail smashed into the carpet of ice balls along their path, exploding into fragments. It was nature's wrath, and they were caught right in the middle of it.

"Mom," Jimmy yelled under the blanket. "What do we do now?"

Lucy glanced at Jimmy. His brilliant blue eyes shone with a courageous resolve, not fear or panic. It was clear his question was merely to figure out the next solution to overcome the newest obstacle in their path. It was then, under nature's icy hellfire, that Lucy realized Adam was right. She *had* shaped the boy's life, and looking at his face was like looking at a reflection of herself. Their connection didn't need to be biological...it was much stronger than just genes. It was soul-deep, forged through years of persistent love, and it radiated brightest now—in the darkest of hours.

Lucy felt energy pour into her veins, rinsing out the insecure doubts she had harbored in her heart. She would never again question their bond.

"Jimmy," Lucy shouted in the deafening pounding, "we must see if..." Her voice cut out.

So too did the racket. The hail stopped as quickly as it had started. It was as if some hand in the sky had turned the faucet off, taking pity on the mortals below.

Lucy and the group slowly lowered the blankets and gazed with astonishment at the wintery landscape spread out before them. An ocean of white spheres filled their eyes. It was like something out of a movie—so aesthetically beautiful, yet so frighteningly shocking. Thousands upon thousands of ice balls covered every inch of the once-green scenery. Colorful flowers had been crushed; other plants had been ripped to shreds and buried or completely enveloped by the hail. It was as if hiding under the blanket had acted like some sort of time machine, transporting the group to a surreal, colorless ice age.

"Whoa…" Randy said, speaking for the kids standing still around him, just as frozen as the trail.

"Oh my goodness," Shannon added. She kicked an ice ball near her shoe, sending it into the air for a few seconds before it landed and disappeared from view.

Lucy turned to the group. "We don't have time to wait around. Those nasty clouds are still over us and can do that again. Follow the footprints of the adults."

Lucy took a step in the thick hail path, but she felt Jimmy grab her arm.

"I have bigger feet, Mom. And more weight to pack the hail down. So does Mr. Newman. It might not be much better, but we should go first."

Lucy nodded without opposition.

Bill started off, followed by Jimmy and Shannon. They stepped in the same footprints, widening the path as best they could for the rest of the group. The kids followed in a straight line behind them.

Lucy decided to hold back again and be the last in the group. It had worked well during the previous two miles; she hoped to repeat that success for the final mile.

CHAPTER 16

The hail never returned. Instead, snow replaced it about fifteen minutes after it ceased. Fat flakes fell at a moderate, steady pace. The snowfall didn't impede the group's progress, nor did it reduce the trail's visibility further, but it did, on occasion, force most of the kids to cover their faces when a sporadic wind gust would whip up and create head-on flurries.

Lucy's shoes and socks were now soaked. Her feet were painfully cold from the hail that had melted on them, creating an unsettling numbness in her toes. It sometimes felt like she was walking on wooden stumps, unable to feel much from her ankle down.

The entire group shared her situation. While most of the children had displayed extraordinary willpower in silently fighting the pain, complaints about the cold and numbness did seep out from a few of the youngest kids who hoped something could be done to immediately alleviate their suffering.

"You'll feel much better once we get to the bus," was Lucy's common response.

Bill and Shannon echoed similar answers.

Jimmy came up with a creative solution to the problem when a first grader named Jennifer started to cry from the agony in her feet. He sang the first children's song that popped in his mind:

Frère Jacques, frère Jacques,
Dormez-vous? Dormez-vous?
Sonnez les matines! Sonnez les matines!
Ding dang dong, ding dang dong.

Jennifer's tears stopped as her eyes lit up, surprised by the song, and she joined in on *Frère Jacques*. Soon the entire group was singing, including the adults. The music diverted their attention and made it seem like they were still on a field trip—a vacation from school, rather than a nightmare in a terrifying forest. They sang the song three times before moving on to *You Are My Sunshine, Row Row Row Your Boat, This Old Man, Twinkle Twinkle Little Star*, and *He's Got the Whole World in His Hands*.

Lucy was astonished by the power of the music. It quickened their pace to almost double what it had been when they were walking in silence. Complaints went the way of the hailstorm, and smiles became contagious—spreading to almost every person in the group.

Lucy thought it was a neat coincidence that they were singing *Wheels on the Bus* right at the moment they finally spotted their bus in the parking lot.

"I see it!" shouted Jennifer, clapping her hands with glee.

The children cut the song short and cheered with wild jubilation—never in their lives had they been so excited to see a school bus. They broke free from the line, running as if in a competition to see who could get to it first.

"Be careful!" Lucy shouted at them, knowing her words would be ignored.

She held her breath while watching them slip and skid along the final thirty feet of the icy trail. Her worry was that a major injury would occur right then, at the last moment when things seemed to be okay. It would be a cruel, ironic twist ending.

But they made it safely. The bus door folded open and out came Gregg with his hands up in the air, expressing as much joy to see them as they were to see him.

"Oh thank God!" Gregg exclaimed. "I was going crazy worrying about you!" He moved aside to let the kids dash into the bus, which he had kept warm by turning the electric engine on and off as needed.

When Lucy finally reached the vehicle, she noticed around a dozen spider cracks in the windshield, and dents all over the hood and side.

Gregg hugged her as if they were best friends.

"Seems you got to experience the same thing we did," Lucy told him, looking at the vehicle's damage.

"Oh, it was the worst hailstorm I've ever been in! By far! I kept thinking about you guys not having the protection I had. It made my stomach sick just picturing those kids trying to get away from it. I prayed you guys found some sort of shelter and waited it out." He furrowed his brow, looking past Lucy. "But where are the rest of the students? Are they close behind you guys?"

"I wish I could say that," Lucy answered. "Kim took the older bunch to Buxton Stream. I have no idea if they made it there, or got wise and turned back."

"Oh no…" Gregg gasped, shaking his head. "That's terrible. What a bad choice that was in this storm."

"Tell us about it," Shannon remarked. "Kim cannot say Lucy didn't warn her."

Gregg waved them inside the bus. "Please, get out of this cold. I'll crank that heater as high as it will go."

Shannon, Bill, and Jimmy entered the bus. Lucy held back for a second, gazing at the contrast of the white landscape set against the dark grey storm. She checked the time.

It was 3:32. That was half an hour past the worst-case scenario that she'd estimated.

CHAPTER 17

Gregg hadn't been kidding. He had blasted the heater so high that the bus became a sauna within minutes. The kids loved it. They were huddled as close to the front as they could get—their shoes and socks removed, their wrinkled feet raised high in the air to unthaw in the blowing heat stream.

Lucy and the others sat in the back, content to have the warmth reach them from afar.

"Is there any way we can make contact with Kim or the students?" Bill asked Gregg. "Reach them somehow to see where they are?"

"If they were in the city, sure. But the forest…not a chance. They have zero reception out there. I've been on that trail before, so I know firsthand. Even this parking lot is in a no-man's zone right now. I haven't gotten a phone signal in hours."

"There's got to be something we can do," Shannon replied. "What if we drive back and get help? Get a snowmobile or something and race out to them?"

Gregg shook his head. "We still get the local stations on the radio, and they all say the same thing. This storm punished everything. The roads are a total mess. Some highways have even been closed."

"I-95?" Bill asked.

"No, thank good God. Not yet. But traffic on it is an absolute parking lot right now. We get on it, we might as well say we are abandoning the others for the night."

"We're not leaving anybody," Lucy fired back.

"I know. Just saying how it is, that's all. We're not going find help unless it finds us. Snowplows and emergency crews are out in force, so maybe help is closer than we think."

Jimmy saw Lucy turn her attention to the storm outside and shake her head. "I know what you're thinking, Mom."

She turned to Jimmy. "Sorry?"

"Dad always said you've never been one to wait around. So I might as well tell you now that I'm going with you. It's too dangerous to go looking alone."

"I was weighing our options," Lucy admitted. "Sitting cozy in this bus while they are out there struggling isn't going to fly with me. They could be really hurt on that trail."

"Where you two go, I go as well," Shannon added. "I'm warm enough now."

Bill's face was a picture of shock. "You guys cannot be serious. Those ice bullets from the sky could return without warning, and even if they don't, you'll still run out of daylight before you make it back. Couple that with the snow coming down, and you'll freeze for sure. Just look at what you have on: t-shirts and shorts."

"I actually have a jacket I stupidly didn't bring when we left," Shannon answered immediately. She dashed to her backpack that she'd stowed away under her seat in the middle of the bus. She unzipped it and removed a windbreaker. She also took out another item and added, "And sweatpants!"

"You can add one more jacket," said Gregg. "Mine's on my seat. I always drive with it, just in case."

"Can I trade my shorts for your pants?" Jimmy asked Gregg, pointing at his blue jeans.

Gregg stared down as if he'd forgotten what he'd put on that morning, then grinned. "Sure. If it helps. We're about the same size."

Jimmy and Gregg quickly made the switch while Shannon retrieved Gregg's jacket, giving it to Lucy to wear.

"There...now we all have at least one warm thing," Shannon said to Bill.

"Don't forget our blankets," Lucy added, handing them to Jimmy while she removed a container of water from her backpack. "Bill, please take this to share with the kids here."

Bill raised an eyebrow. "You don't need this?"

"I've got plenty of water left for us on the trail; I packed way more than needed before I left the house this morning. I have a habit of preparing for the worst. Guess it's just in my nature, given all the things I've been through."

"I have a hard time believing you've seen anything like that before...what we experienced out there."

Lucy gave Bill a thin smile. "It's a long, long story. We'll save it for another day." She turned to Gregg. "Please keep checking your reception and see if you can get a signal. We need to get outside help as soon as possible."

"Yes, ma'am," Gregg promised. "Oh! And take these snacks with you before you go." Gregg led Lucy and her team to the front of the bus, where he opened a small cooler and removed two large bags of shelled peanuts.

He gave them to Jimmy and said, "They're great for protein. I hope you guys don't have allergies."

"Mom and I are fine. Shannon?"

Shannon opened the bag in front of Jimmy, grabbed a dozen peanuts, and tossed them in her mouth. "What do you think, Jimbo?"

Jimmy laughed. "Um, yes. Deathly allergic, I see."

"Let's go, you two," Lucy said. She then turned to the kids sitting around them, still thawing off from the cold. "Everyone listen! Some of the adults need to leave to look for the rest of our group. But Gregg and Bill will still be with you guys, and soon we will all get out of here."

"I'm hungry," came a complaint from one of the kids.

"Me too," said Jennifer. "When can we eat?"

"Well…" Lucy began, before she felt Gregg's hand on her shoulder.

"Don't worry about it," Gregg said softly to her. "I've got more snacks I can share with them. But take this. Bill has a good point about the daylight; it won't stick around forever." He handed Lucy a small flashlight from inside the dash console.

Lucy took it, gave him a quick hug, and made her way out. Shannon and Jimmy followed her.

Right as Jimmy reached the door, Randy ran to him. "I want to go, too!"

Jimmy stopped and faced him, bending down to his level. "Wish you could, buddy, but it's going to be dangerous out there. Even for somebody my size."

"I can handle danger!" Randy protested.

Jimmy smiled at him. "I know you can. All magicians can brave the worst of dangers. But I want you to practice that card trick I showed you this morning. You remember how it was done, right?"

Randy nodded.

"Good," Jimmy said, sticking out his hand so Randy could slap it—which he did.

"So you'll be back soon? You're not going to go home in another bus without us, right?"

Jimmy stared directly in Randy's deep brown eyes, recalling the promise that had been made and kept when he was Randy's age.

"I will never leave you."

CHAPTER 18

Lucy, Jimmy, and Shannon walked as fast as they could along the hail-blanketed trail. They'd left the bus just after four o'clock, and the wind had kicked up significantly in the forty minutes it took them to reach the spot where they had stopped in the storm during the worst of the ice torrent. Gusts whipped snow against their faces. The flurries also covered the footprints they had made earlier, making it difficult to retrace their exact path and avoid stepping off the boardwalk.

Then there was the light: flat, fading. It was an ever-present reminder that the day was slowly slipping away, that the night would soon swallow them and significantly hinder their rescue efforts.

"See anybody, Jimmy?" Lucy said loudly in the wind, looking back at her son as she led the way. "Your eyes are better than mine."

"No," Jimmy yelled, gazing as far ahead as the trail would permit. "No one."

"Do you guys think they might have taken a different route back?" Shannon asked from behind Jimmy. "Maybe they found another way that was easier."

Lucy stopped for a moment, considered the question, then shook her head. "The trail does eventually loop, but taking the other way doesn't make any sense. It's more than twice as long back to the bus going that direction. Kim would have known that. So would the seniors."

"It's possible they made their own path," said Jimmy. "They might have thought they could make better time. Or maybe they accidently wandered off the trail because of all this hail and snow."

"We're really in trouble if that's the case," Lucy replied. "We have no choice but to assume they are still in front of us, despite how far we've backtracked. Let's keep going."

They continued on. As they walked, a rabbit bolted across their path in a blur. It was gone so fast that had it not been for the paw prints it left behind in the snow, Lucy would have questioned whether she had really seen it at all.

It was the only animal they had seen in several hours. The absence of wildlife was both eerie and ominous, a warning signal that commanded them to seek the protection of shelter or suffer the consequences for their foolish choices. The blame for those choices was irrelevant. Mother Nature didn't care. You either abided by her rules or you found out the hard way that her laws were universal and unbendable.

Lucy's right foot slipped as she stepped on a large hail ball, rolling her weight on her ankle. She yelled out as she took a hard fall in the ice and snow.

"Mom!" Jimmy cried out, reaching down for her. He grabbed under her arms and tried lifting her, but Lucy didn't stand.

"Hold on, Jimmy…."

"I saw what happened. Did you sprain your ankle?"

Lucy shook her head. "Don't think so. Just hurts like hell. Give me a second."

"Hey! Guys!" Shannon said. "See that over there?" Shannon pointed at two trees roughly seventy yards off. Between them, a group of people inched forward in the snow.

"Yeah! I do!" Jimmy replied.

"Same here," Lucy said, grabbing Jimmy's hand to hoist herself back up. She grunted as she stood, putting as much weight as she could on her good foot.

"Can you see how many there are?" Shannon asked.

"They are too far away and too close together," Jimmy said. "Still, it doesn't seem like it's all of them."

"It isn't," Lucy replied. "No way that could be. Damn. Something must have happened."

CHAPTER 19

Lucy, Jimmy, and Shannon listened intently to the students.

"It came from all directions. It started small at first, and most of us just laughed and jogged to get out of the way. Like it was some game. But it got ugly fast. I mean really fast. It started to sting, and then hurt like the devil. It got so bad that it felt like we were getting hit with stones. Our laughs became screams as we panicked. I just ran like everyone else with my hands guarding my face. You see, there was no cover anywhere..."

Peter Mills stopped his story and stared at his bruised and bloodied hands. His eighteen-year-old face looked like it had been through a twelve-round boxing match—one which he had clearly lost. One eye was swollen and caked with blood to the point that he couldn't see out of it. When he held out his hands, his right index finger looked so jagged and battered that Lucy was certain it was broken.

The other students were just as banged up. It was as if they were in a play or movie, and they had just finished applying the last touches on their gory makeup. It seemed unreal watching them as they shivered in the blanket Jimmy and Shannon had wrapped around the group.

"We were in the worst place imaginable," said a petite senior named Cindy. "Buxton Stream is right in the center of this huge meadow. Some areas are flat and some are sort of hilly, but there's not a single tree. I never bothered to notice that fact when we were going over there. I just enjoyed the flowers we saw—taking in the pretty stuff, you know? But running through that hail was a whole different story. I kept thinking, where are the trees? Where are the trees?"

Lucy shifted her gaze from Cindy to Peter, then to the five other senior students huddled around them. She refrained from asking them whether they had remembered the two blankets she had given to them; it was now a moot point. Either Kim had failed to get them out of her bag, or the fever of the panic had clouded their judgment to use them as protective covers.

"Where are Kim and the others?" Lucy asked the group, her eyes on Peter and Cindy. "Are they behind you guys?" Lucy already sensed the answer to her own question, but she was hoping her gut was wrong.

"I ran all the way back to the campground," Peter explained. "So did Cindy, and everyone else who's here. We waited for more to show, but no one did. It seemed like forever in that cold."

"It really did," Cindy cut in. "I guess it was only half an hour or so looking back on it, but we just couldn't stick around forever. We should have left when you guys did, Lucy. I kept thinking that again and again."

"Is it...is it far?" said one senior, his teeth chattering. "The ba-bus?"

"Just a little bit more," Lucy replied. "You should get there before the daylight completely dies out." She turned around. "Shannon, I want you to go with them and lead the way back. I'm not taking any risks on kids getting lost again. It's too easy to do, even with our footprints in the trail."

"What about you and Jimmy?" Shannon asked.

"We'll continue to the campground and onward if needed. We'll search for as long as we can take it."

Shannon turned to Jimmy. "You'll be in the dark. You won't be able to see a thing out there in the woods."

Lucy took out the flashlight Gregg had given to her. "We'll have some help. Not much, but it will do."

"I hate to leave you two to go out alone. Are you sure about this?"

Jimmy smiled at Shannon and put his hand on her arm. "Mom and I have always found a way out of fixes. We'll be fine."

He hugged her. When he pulled back, Shannon planted a quick kiss on his lips. She quickly turned around before he could react to it, leading her group home.

Lucy watched them head off, then smiled at Jimmy. "I think you've got a new girlfriend, sweetie," she said, elbowing her son.

"Who? Shannon? No."

"Just saying, Jimmy. Women know these things."

Jimmy laughed while Lucy looked down at her foot and took a step to test it.

"Are you going to be okay, Mom? Maybe you should head back with them."

"I'm fine. It's already a little better. We'll take it slow so I can walk it off."

"Okay. You go first, then."

Lucy did, hobbling slightly as she went.

Jimmy trailed his mother, looking over his shoulder every so often to watch Shannon and her group slowly fade from view.

The storm clouds were a soupy, indistinguishable dark grey. They were heavily pregnant with precipitation, which continued to make its way down in the form of snow. The flakes were now much smaller than they had been earlier, and dropped to the ground much more quickly. They seemed to come from all angles in the frequent gusts, as if their source was something other than the storm itself.

Lucy and Jimmy shielded their faces against a fierce flurry blowing directly against them. It grew stronger, churning up so much snow that they disappeared in a swirling white funnel.

The time was 5:10.

Chapter 20

Lucy had thought the day couldn't get any stranger, but when she saw the campground in what would be the last natural light before the dawn of evening, she swore she was looking at a place she'd never seen. The ground, tables, benches, trashcans, porta-potties—all of it was frosted in white. It was if they had jumped seasons in the span of six hours.

"Just look at it," Lucy said softly, one hand close to her mouth in shock. "I can't believe this is where we had lunch."

"Wow, that is crazy," said Jimmy, standing still beside his mother and absorbing the scene. "Not a single sign of anyone, either. I was hoping this would be the end… That we could finally get them and turn back."

"That makes two of us. I thought we'd find them by now. I'm afraid something really bad must have happened. It's the only thing that makes sense."

"Why else stick around in this hell?"

"Exactly."

"What now? Do we risk going on, now that it's night?"

"I hate to say yes. To be honest, it scares me a little thinking we will be venturing further out with just one flashlight. We have nothing else, not even extra batteries. Can you imagine if the flashlight goes dead?"

"We'd be in total darkness. No help from the moon or stars. Do you really think that will happen?"

"Not really. The odds are in our favor for once." She turned the flashlight on. The whiteness of the snow burst like a firework in the cone-shaped beam.

The light supremely illuminated the continuing snowfall in the otherwise invisible night storm.

"It's not flickering or getting dim, so that's a good thing."

"That's my thought," Lucy agreed. "I think the best plan is to treat it like we don't have much left, and keep moving as fast as we can."

"Which way is the other trail?"

Lucy pointed the flashlight around the campground. She settled on a picnic table at the far end of the campground. "There, behind that table. I remember seeing it when we came for lunch. We should see a trail marker next to it. Let's go."

She pushed forward. The pain in her ankle was mostly gone, allowing her to move faster.

Jimmy noticed her quickened pace and matched it. He wondered what Randy was doing at that same moment, and whether Shannon and her group had now joined them in the bus.

It was possible, he thought. If so, they'd made it just in time to avoid the perils of night that now faced those who were lost, and those who were out seeking them.

CHAPTER 21

Lucy kept her flashlight fixed on the footprints, following the only evidence she had of the buried trail. It wasn't easy. The falling snow nearly concealed many of the tracks left behind by Peter, Cindy, and the other seniors. What had started out as a clear route to the meadow had quickly transformed into an indistinguishable white sheet of powder.

Jimmy walked by her side so they could both utilize the blanket they had brought. The extra layer made a world of difference against the evening gusts, which were still blowing head-on in a strong assault to their progress. Some flurries were so violent that they had no choice but to stop and wait them out. The longest of these squalls seriously pit their pain against their endurance and patience, as if testing the depths of their tenacity.

"Why can't we take all those blistering record days we had last summer and use them to offset this weather?" Jimmy asked rhetorically.

"It would be nice, wouldn't it?" Lucy replied, shielding her face from yet another gust.

"Do you think singing more songs will make this any easier?"

Lucy laughed. "I think that trick only works when we have an enthusiastic chorus. Duets won't cut it. But talking helps divert the mind, so keep at it. The subject doesn't matter."

"What was the name of that distant relative on my mom's side of the family you told me about? The singer. The one you discovered when going through the adoption?"

"Um...Ellie something. Ellie Brook, I think it was."

"You said she was big way back during the turn of the millennium?"

"Yes, but I'm not sure how *big* she made it though. Most of her shows were in small jazz clubs around New Orleans. Local stuff. I just saw this short newspaper blurb about it when digging through your family history."

"Wow, things must have really been different way back in those days. What do you think her world was like? Think she saw this kind of stuff?"

"Climate-wise, you mean? Not as extreme as we are seeing it now. But Ellie knew. They all knew, even back then. They saw the beginning signs of the global changes."

A massive gust ripped through the forest trees, hitting Lucy and Jimmy hard, forcing them to stop and seek protection under their blanket. They felt like the wind would knock them over if it grew any stronger.

It died down after a long thrashing, and they carried on through the passage.

"If you could write a letter to the past, say around Ellie's time, what would you say?" Jimmy asked.

"A note? You mean if I got to pass on what I know of the present to people that were alive back then?"

"Basically. Just a message that they would take to heart. Have it go viral with the technology they had at the time so everyone would pay attention."

They walked in silence for a long moment, Lucy lost in thought. "I don't know, Jimmy," she finally said. "I'd have to think really hard about what I wanted that letter to say. I know the tone of it wouldn't be damning or accusatory. It'd be more of a call to action. To do something for future generations."

"Good answer."

"How about you? What would you say?"

"Dear fucking self-centered bastards..."

The words hit Lucy like a sack of bricks against her chest. She immediately froze. "Jimmy!"

Jimmy laughed. "I'm kidding, Mom. Of course I wouldn't say that to them."

"I need to wash out that dirty mouth of yours. I've never heard you swear like that before!"

"Well, I learned it from Dad."

Lucy's stern face broke into a smile. "Yes, I can see that coming from your father. But still...no more language like that, young man."

"It got your mind off the cold, didn't it?"

Lucy laughed. She wouldn't admit that it had, or that she appreciated Jimmy for that much-needed relief.

The trees eventually thinned out, giving way to a path of absolute whiteness as far as their limited light could penetrate. It was devoid of shape or form. It was like looking at a barren, frozen moon—one where life had never had the chance to take root and thrive.

As they entered the amorphous expanse, Jimmy spoke again to his mother, "This must be the meadow they mentioned. We're getting close."

"I hope so. It all depends on if they stayed in this area and didn't wander off, so that our search—"

Lucy's voice died in her throat. Her mouth remained as still and silent as her feet, and Jimmy mirrored her motionlessness—staring with bulging eyes at the remarkable creature in front of them. It was a bull moose of extraordinary size. Its height was just shy of seven feet; its muscular weight approached half a ton. Broad, palmate antlers with elaborate tines along the edge protruded proudly from either side of its bulky head. Its body was positioned lengthwise, as if on display in the beam of Lucy's flashlight.

Its face was parallel to its frozen stance, staring ahead without the slightest interest in the new company in its midst.

"Whoa, I didn't think these existed anymore arou—" Jimmy whispered before Lucy pinched his arm, cutting him off.

"Shhhh," Lucy said in the lowest voice possible.

The wind bent their voices to the animal, causing it to glance in their direction. Watching the full glory of its antlers rotate into view was a show in itself. The bone extensions couldn't have been more prominent and symmetrical, a true symbol of a mature bull whose physical and sexual prowess was certain to attract whatever mate crossed its path.

And yet, Lucy thought, who were its mates? Jimmy's question was on the tip of her tongue, too: how on Earth had this creature found its way this far down south? American moose, with the exception of those in Alaska and the northern forests of Washington State, had migrated to Canada in search of more hospitable habitats. Lucy remembered seeing a picture of one years ago in Jimmy's fifth-grade class. A student's great-grandfather had been hiking in Baxter State Park (in the center of Maine) and had snapped a quick photo of a moose he'd spotted near Mt. Katahdin. The image caused such a stir that it made the school paper.

Ironically, the one in front of Lucy and Jimmy seemed twice as large and magnificent, and no one but them would know about it.

Lucy's heart pounded inside her chest. She barely breathed, feeling the slightest noise from her lips would send the animal bolting.

Jimmy's wide blue eyes reflected the same feelings. His petrified posture—an arm slightly jutted out, a knee bent in mid-stride—would have impressed the most skilled of mimes. He was his own wax double—the perfect candidate for a portrait artist.

The moment seemed to last hours for Lucy and Jimmy, but in truth it was only about a minute. The moose focused on the route ahead and trotted off with stiff legs into the darkness. It vanished the same way it had appeared, as if in a dream, leaving behind only the memory of its splendor etched on the minds of two admiring witnesses.

"Wow!" Jimmy said after a long pause. "Did we just see that?"

"I wouldn't believe it if you hadn't seen it with me. That moose was beyond describing."

"It was huge! Like a moving tank. It's funny, but I wasn't scared about it charging us. I should have been, I guess."

"I know what you mean; I had the same feeling. It was just curious about us. Nothing more, really. I don't think I've seen anything so beautiful in my life before."

"Shoot...and no picture or video of it, either."

"Yes, but those wouldn't do it justice anyway."

"Heeelloooo!" shouted a far-off voice in the darkness. "Over here!"

Lucy's face snapped towards the direction of the shout. She aimed her flashlight in the darkness. She didn't see anyone at first, sweeping her beam around in wide arcs as if her ears had deceived her.

Then Jimmy grabbed her hand and stopped it at a fixed point. "There, Mom!"

Lucy squinted her eyes, barely seeing two distant figures at the end of her faded light. They were waving their hands above their heads. It was as if they were trying to signal a plane on a deserted island.

Lucy had one thought upon seeing them: *Where were the rest?*

CHAPTER 22

Nelson Chambers did all the talking while Seth Roth stood beside him, shivering. They were both eighteen, but Nelson was much taller and bulkier than his friend; thus, he was better able to handle the extreme conditions.

Nelson repeated many of the same facts that Peter and Cindy had given: the laughter in the first moments of the hailstorm, the terrified panic that sunk in when the ice begin to hurt and they found themselves without shelter in the open meadow, the swelling confusion in the immediate aftermath. In the beam of Lucy's flashlight Nelson and Seth looked just as bruised and cut as the other seniors—maybe even worse.

"Half of us were missing when we regrouped," Nelson said, his lips purple from the cold. "And that's when we found out it was really bad. Someone broke their leg."

"What?" Lucy asked. "Who? Kim?"

Nelson shook his head. "No, a senior. Heather Page. It's really terrible. It happened when she was running. She got her foot caught in a hole. It snapped when she fell."

"Where is she?" Jimmy asked. "Why are you guys separated from them?"

"We waited for hours just sitting around doing nothing. We hoped the other seniors would return, or that you guys would come looking for us sooner. Had Kim been in a better state, she might have told us what to do when things got bad. Eventually we had no choice but to pick two people to go out and look for help. That was us."

"You said it was Heather who broke her leg?" Lucy asked, confused. "What do you mean by Kim being in a better state?"

"It's best you see for yourself. I don't know what happened to her, honestly. It's really strange."

"Show us the way," Lucy replied. "We better hurry."

"Seth, you're better at following tracks than me. You okay to lead?" Nelson asked.

Seth nodded with his arms crossed so tightly around his chest it seemed he'd squeeze himself to death. Despite his affirmation, it was hard to tell if he'd tip over like a statue, remaining frozen for the duration of the storm, or if he'd really be able to put one foot in front of the other and lead the way.

He managed to pull off the latter, taking the flashlight. Lucy, Jimmy, and Nelson followed behind.

CHAPTER 23

It took a little longer than Lucy had expected for them to hike back to the group. She wondered how Nelson and Seth could have wandered so far off without turning back and declaring their search mission a lost cause (especially when the light of day slipped into the blindness of night). She suspected that Nelson and Seth had become lost themselves when it became too late to turn back. Their relief at spotting her and Jimmy certainly supported such a supposition.

Seth finally came to a stop in front of a large boulder. He aimed the flashlight at it and performed a cursory inspection while standing twenty feet away. He then nodded to Nelson.

"This is it," Nelson said flatly.

"What do you mean?" Lucy asked. "I don't see anybody."

"We took cover on the other side of it. It provided a little better protection from the storm."

Seth took them around the yacht-sized rock, stopping at a makeshift shelter which had been made using Lucy's two brown blankets. There wasn't much to it: a few sticks for support and four heavy stones to weigh down the corners against the wind.

It would have been very easy to pass it by, Lucy thought, thankful that she had Seth and Nelson to show them the location. The blankets practically blended into the boulder itself.

Seth handed the flashlight back to Lucy; she took it and poked her head inside. She saw Kim's face first—red nose and cheeks, disheveled hair, glazed eyes fixed straight ahead in a vacant stare. Kim was seated between two female seniors, who immediately looked up at Lucy and jumped to their feet to hug her.

"Oh thank God!" one girl said, embracing Lucy so hard she had difficulty breathing. "Thank you! Thank you!"

"You came back!" said the other girl, joining in with her arms wrapped around Lucy's waist, crying. "We'd given up all hope!"

"It's okay, girls. You have help now."

Lucy had to wait a second before they stepped aside, revealing three senior boys sitting around Heather, who was lying supine with both hands on her injured leg. Lucy moved to them, ducking under the blanket roof as best she could.

"Hi Heather, how are you holding up?"

Heather's eyes revealed her pain and exhaustion; they were slightly bloodshot and droopy—but Lucy thought she was doing rather well, considering the circumstances.

"It hurts a lot," Heather said in a slow voice, glancing at her leg. "I'm such a dummy. I'm the reason we all got stuck here. We'd be fine if—"

"Quiet, you," Lucy said, cutting her off. "Accidents make the rounds with all of us. Today was just your day, nothing more."

Lucy hunkered down and aimed the light at the break in Heather's leg, finding a closed, displaced fracture of her tibia five inches below her knee. While the fractured bone had not broken the skin, it was noticeably pushing against it. It looked like a blunt knife was trying to cut its way out of her limb.

"You did a good job breaking it, that's for sure. Too bad we don't have an award for that at the school."

A soft laugh escaped Heather's mouth for a second, then was immediately replaced by a wincing cry.

"Sorry. I don't want to make you feel more pain. We need to get you to someone who can look at this properly." Lucy faced the others. "She'll never make it limping between two of us, and if we picked a person to carry her, he'd never make it the full distance without stumbling and dropping her on that trail of ice."

"Then what do we do, Mom?"

Lucy's eyes shifted to where her son was peeking his head through a part in the blankets. It felt bizarre looking at him that way, and seeing the others staring, too; it was as if they were overgrown kids playing a game of fort.

"We will make a stretcher using what few items we have with us. It won't be pretty, but it will be much better than trying to do without it."

"How?" one of the seniors next to Heather asked. "We don't have rope or tape or anything useful. Wait...did you guys bring some with you?"

"No, but that's okay," Lucy replied. "These blankets combined with these sticks you collected to prop them up will do more than you can imagine if we put them together right. We just have to make sure they're aligned."

"Are you sure?" Heather asked with fear in her eyes.

Lucy could sense her mixed feelings of wanting to get the hell out of the woods, but also not wanting to go through more agony in the process. Lucy gave Heather a comforting smile. "I used to work with a rescue organization many years ago. They taught us a few skills for emergency situations like this, and I still remember most of what I learned. It's been awhile, like I said, but we'll get this done. Jimmy...I need your help, along with Nelson's."

"What do you want us to do, Mom?"

For some reason Lucy couldn't explain, she glanced at Kim for a second. Kim's eyes were still glued in an empty gaze in front of her. Lucy recalled how different she had been at the start of the trip, how confident (borderline cocky) she'd been while directing the group.

While some might have felt a sense of poetic justice for how the situation had turned against Kim (due in part to her own misjudgments), the emotion flowing through Lucy's veins was not one of delight, but sadness. She wanted Kim to come out of it, to understand that her mistake was now in the past and that her leadership was still needed in the present.

True strength, true love is in mercy. Forgiveness is the core of human growth.

"Mom?" Jimmy repeated, furrowing his brow. "What do we do?"

The memory of Grandma Clara's voice vanished, and Lucy fixed her focus back on her son. "Take down these blankets and find the two longest and straightest sticks we have. We must move quickly."

CHAPTER 24

One branch was close to perfect for the job. It bent only slightly at the end, and the rest of it was straight and sturdy. The second branch had its share of flaws: it was crooked, a bit short, and a little too skinny for comfort. However, their options were limited, and they had no choice but to use it.

Lucy guided the group to lay the two blankets on top of each other for the best support. She then instructed them to put the straightest branch in the middle and fold the blankets over it. The second stick came in next, about shoulder width from the first one, again on top of the blankets. They folded the covers the opposite way, leaving just the ends of the branches exposed.

"Those are our handles," Lucy said, illuminating them with the flashlight.

"Won't it just come undone when we lift it?" Nelson asked.

"Not when she lays in it," came a soft reply.

It was from Seth Roth. A surprised Lucy and the group turned to him, amazed that words had actually penetrated his lips.

"Seth's right," Lucy affirmed. "Heather's weight will keep it in place and prevent it from unfolding. The trick now is to get her in as easily as we can. Let's slide this right beside her."

Lucy did so with the help of the group.

"Jimmy and Nelson, on my signal I want you two to gently left Heather under her arms and move her on. I will get her by her good leg and Seth will make sure her broken one doesn't get caught under her when she comes back down. You guys got it?"

They nodded at her.

Lucy gave the flashlight to one of the girls in the group and moved into position.

Heather's eyes were as wide as saucers. "I'm scared."

"It will be nice and quick, Heather. I promise. Like removing a Band-Aid."

Lucy slid her right arm under the knee of Heather's good leg and used her free hand to help lift Heather's back.

"Okay boys, on three... One, two, three."

Heather cried loudly in pain as they raised her up and moved her atop the stretcher, setting her down swiftly but gently.

Lucy was worried that if they'd put her too close to either edge of the stretcher, they'd have to reposition her again. On inspection, she was relieved to see they'd put her in the proper spot, avoiding further complications.

"Nelson and Jimmy, I want you two to carry it. If you get tired, let me know and I'll rotate you guys out. You know how to hold it, right?"

"We both face forward," Jimmy replied. "Not facing each other like we are carrying a table or sofa."

"That's right. That shorter stick will make things interesting, so keep a good grip on it. I'm crossing my fingers that we won't have to replace it." She covered Heather with one of her blankets, and then turned to the group, who were taking turns using the second blanket Lucy had carried. It was currently wrapped around Seth and two of the girls. "Is everyone ready?"

They said they were as a strong gust of wind shot against them. Lucy guarded her face from it, then walked up to Kim after it faded.

"Kim, are you set, too?"

Her eyes seemed to look right through Lucy, staring into some dark abyss. She nodded without any facial cues that she understood what was going on.

Lucy wanted to say more to her, to see if she could reach inside and flip on the lights, but she didn't have the time. "Okay. Home we go."

CHAPTER 25

It was as if the storm seemed to know the end was near and did its best to make it as difficult as possible for Lucy and the students to make their way back. The wind was stronger and the gusts became more frequent. The footprint trails were nearly erased as a result, forcing Jimmy, who was at the head of the line, to pause several times to make sure he was following the correct route. Seth stood beside him, lighting the path.

Lucy remained at the rear of the group, just behind Kim. She shouted words of encouragement whenever the wind forced their progress to a standstill, telling them to keep their spirits up and carry on as if they only had a few steps left to go.

Heather moaned in agony during the most powerful of flurries. Her cries were loud enough for even Lucy to hear at the opposite end—terrible groans that were blacker than the hidden forest, more unnerving than the looming, unrelenting storm.

Lucy hadn't bothered to check the hour when they had left, and by now she had completely lost track of time altogether. She had no idea if it had taken thirty minutes or an hour and a half to reach the campground. The same was true when they passed the spot where Shannon had taken the first group of students back. Lucy knew all the rest stops along the way had eaten up a significant portion of time, but how much time exactly was a mystery that she didn't care to find out. The present moment was all that was important. Step by step. Breath by breath. Her only goal was to get these kids back without any further physical harm, and she didn't give a damn if it took her three hours or all night to do the job.

"Jimmy...aren't you and Nelson tired?" Lucy shouted to the front of the group after another bitter storm blast—which had forced the group to a halt—had petered out.

"We're fine, Mom. We've got it."

"You don't have to carry her the whole way. Others can help."

"We know. Don't worry about us."

The group started to move again.

Lucy's mouth curved into a thin smile that no one saw in the darkness. She pictured herself in Jimmy's shoes, likely doing the exact same thing. Stubbornness ran strong in the family—even when there wasn't a biological connection.

"It was my fault..."

Lucy barely heard the words, and even questioned if her mind was playing tricks on her at such a late hour in the day. But then she heard the voice again.

"This was *all my fault*."

It came from Kim. Lucy could only see her vague silhouette in the dark— what she'd been following to keep pace with the line—but she knew Kim was looking back at her when she said it.

"Kim, nobody knew this would happen. Not like this. And it doesn't matter now anyway. That's behind us."

Kim started to cry. It began as a soft whimper, then slid into a loud and deep wailing. Lucy embraced her. Kim put her head on her shoulder and sobbed in her arms, shaking as her pent-up emotions poured out.

"Her leg, Lucy. Heather's poor, terrible le—"

"Shhhh..." Lucy whispered as if Kim were a child.

"Is everything okay?" came a male voice in the dark in front of them.

"We're fine," Lucy replied. "Just releasing some stress, that's all."

The unseen person didn't inquire further, shifting his focus elsewhere.

Kim remained in Lucy's arms for a short moment longer, then pulled back, sniffling. "She's going to be okay, right? Heather and the rest of us?"

"Yes, of course. Just a little bit more and we will be safe."

It was Lucy's only lie that day. She deeply wanted her promise to be true, for their nightmare to come to a swift end, but to say she knew with certainty that it would conclude so quickly was like saying she knew what the storm would cook up for them along the way. The danger ahead was still very real—from wandering off course, to freezing in a bout of brutal gusts, to Heather dying because of a blood clot.

It was a fib Lucy had to tell not only to Kim, but to herself. She needed hope on the unforeseen path, faith in the journey's conclusion.

"I'm sorry, Lucy. I'm sorry and I thank you."

"Hold on before you say the thanks," Lucy replied. "No giving me that until I've actually proven myself. I don't deserve it yet."

"Yes you do. For so many things already, especially building that stretcher out of nothing. I did pay attention, you know. Do you think it will hold the rest of the way?"

"I'm crossing my fingers. It seems to be doing the trick so far, but I don't want to jinx myself."

"Hey! You guys better keep up!" came the same male voice that had questioned Lucy.

"Sorry!" Lucy said, noting that the group was moving again. She put a hand on Kim's back, slightly pushing her. "Go ahead of me. I like to be the last car in the train."

"To push broken engines like me?" Kim asked, starting to walk.

"Not broken. Only needing a little oil."

As they started to walk, an astonishing opening in the clouds appeared. It was small, not much larger than the size of a full moon if one had been there to fill the hole, and in it Lucy caught the clearest, brightest stars she could ever recall filling her eyes. It was like a window to heaven, a sparkling paradise piercing through, and contrasting against, the ceaseless black tempest.

Lucy kept her gaze on it as she followed the group, wondering how far those distant suns were from Earth, and whether some member of an intelligent species could be looking her direction and wondering the same thoughts. It made her feel indescribably small—an ant in the grand opera of the cosmos.

How strange our universe is, she thought. How beautifully strange.

CHAPTER 26

12:22 pm.

That was the exact time when Lucy's foot touched the bus, marking the end to her eight-hour rescue mission. No one bothered to record the specific minute it happened. The outbreak of cheers and joyous emotions took control of all thoughts and senses, intoxicating the group far faster than any consumed substance could ever come close to achieving. Even the youngest students, who had fallen asleep in the interim, awoke to the commotion with wide eyes and bewildered smiles—looking as if they hadn't been resting, but rather playing a game to fool others into thinking they were dreaming.

Gregg had informed Lucy that he'd reached outside help, and that aid, though long overdue (a fact he cursed about several times), was expected soon.

Lucy's legs felt like rubber, but before taking a seat to rest her fatigued body, she walked over to Heather at the back of the bus. Jimmy and Nelson left her in the stretcher on the floor of the center aisle because she would need to be removed on it when the time came to get her out.

"I've never broken a bone before," Heather admitted to Lucy, a blanket under her head serving as a pillow. "Not even sprained something or had stitches. Nothing."

"I guess there's a first time for everything," Lucy said, kneeling beside her. She took a quick look at the wound, then covered it back up. "You did wonderfully, Heather. I'm proud of you."

"Me? Yeah, sure. All I did was lay like a stupid dummy. We would have been back hours ago had it not been for me."

"Or not back at all. It's impossible to know why fate steers us down the path we must take. I was taught at an early age that things happen for a reason."

"You think that's really true?"

Lucy thought about what her grandma had told her out on the patio, about her destiny. She then thought about how she met Adam and Jimmy. "In my life, yes. I truly do." Lucy grabbed Heather's hand, squeezed it, and made for the closest empty seat.

She collapsed in it, her eyes snapping shut almost immediately. The storm and its fury vanished from her consciousness, and in its place, in her first dream, was a clear night sky speckled with an ocean of stars. The distant suns filled every corner of her weary mind.

PART IV
EARTH

CHAPTER 27

"Just sit tight for a second. Keep looking straight at the camera. We need a few stills before we can start."

"I was told this would be quick," Lucy shot back at the director, squinting her eyes in the bright lights. "You're putting more grey in my hair, making me wait around like this."

"You look beautiful, Lucy. Ageless. I couldn't find a single strand of grey to begin with."

"Flattery will get you nowhere, young man. I've seen and heard it all, so don't you try to play me for a fool."

Lucy heard a quick burst of clicks, then saw Steven, the director of the documentary, motion to a crew member to fix a reflector angled at Lucy's back.

"This studio is a bit tiny for this project, wouldn't you say?" Lucy asked, glancing around a space no larger than a bedroom. She was thankful claustrophobia didn't run in her blood, for if it did, she would have bolted out in horror.

"I can control all the elements precisely the way I need them," Steven replied, eyes focused on his camera. "Even if I had a larger budget, I'd still pick this place. The results speak for themselves."

"Well, to be honest I didn't care very much for your prior two documentaries. The one on outsourced farming and the other on the benefits of tariffs. They both seemed like you had an agenda to prove no matter what facts were piled atop that fat bald head of yours."

Steven's face popped up from behind the camera, his eyes wide with surprise. "Really? Why on earth did you agree to help with this project, then? If you really feel that way?"

Deep crow's feet formed at the corners of Lucy's hazel eyes as her lips creased into a smile. "Because I have a good gut instinct about things, and I think you are finally going to get one film right. It's a numbers game. You can't mess them all up. Even a fool wins every once in a while."

Steven stared blankly at Lucy for moment, then shook his head and laughed. "Lucy Gold... You are something else. They warned me about you before this interview. They said you'd grown feisty in your older years. I was told to bring a shield and expect hellfire if I set off your sharp wit."

"I thought I was ageless?"

"You are, and always will be in my mind. I found out a lot about you while I was doing research for this project. I know about your childhood in California, your work with the Rescue Ravens in Louisiana, and your heroic act of saving those kids in Maine."

"That ancient Bangor News article is rubbish. It was all of us that pulled together to get out of that mess, not just me alone. I told that reporter not to write it that way, and he still did. It made me seem like some superhero, which I assure you I am not." She pursed her lips at Steven and narrowed her gaze. "Please tell me you're not taking that angle in this film. I was told I'd be one of many. That this was a story of climate change migration as seen through the lives of ordinary Americans."

"It will be, Lucy. I give you my word on it."

"That's not encouraging."

Steven grinned. "I suppose not. But you are only one of two dozen I will be interviewing. I just want to trace the places you've been, what you experienced during your stay, and your reasons for moving. My hope is that a larger picture will unfold as I piece these stories together, showing a compilation of the geographic and socioeconomic changes that are manifesting all over the globe, not just in our country."

"Good," Lucy said, adjusting a hair tie behind her head to hold in place her long, peppered strands. "That is something in which I'd like to participate."

"Are you ready to begin?"

"Say the word."

"Okay. First, please look directly at the camera and say your name."

Chapter 28

Lucy didn't watch the completed product of Steven's documentary, a film entitled *South to North*. One of her reasons was that she wanted to avoid seeing herself on screen. She felt the experience would be too bizarre and awkward—a feeling supported by her unsettled reaction to simply spotting her name in the paper when skimming an article about the movie.

But another reason, a stronger one, was that she didn't want to be disappointed by the result. She felt her heart would break if Steven had failed to capture the spine of the story, either by intention or accident. She was too close to the subject matter; her life had been molded by it. Lucy trusted her gut instinct that Steven would get it right, but she didn't care to put that intuition to the test.

She carried on with her retired life in Bangor—cooking Cajun and southwestern food for her family, reading classic novels, painting watercolor flowers, and playing with her five-year-old granddaughter. Susan, or Susie as everyone called her, looked more like Shannon than Jimmy. She had green eyes, a slightly cleft chin, well-defined cheekbones, and shiny blonde hair that almost looked like locks of gold when the sun shone on it.

Lucy was teaching Susie how to juice an orange by hand one Saturday afternoon when a knock came at her front door.

"Grandma, someone's outside," Susie said, standing on the tips of her toes to peer out through the kitchen window. "I'll get it!" Susie excitedly raced off, her yellow dress billowing behind her.

Lucy wiped her sticky hands on her apron, furrowing her brow. She wasn't expecting company. Adam, Jimmy, and Shannon had gone to a baseball game; they weren't due back for several hours.

Susie turned the door handle without hesitation.

Concerned, Lucy shouted, "Susie, hold on! Don't just—"

But it was already too late—the door was wide open, revealing a woman with white hair, soft eyes, and a face crumpled with wrinkles so deep they looked like cracks on a dried-up lakebed. She stood still as rock in a red t-shirt and faded blue jeans.

She looked lost. Confused.

"May I help you?" Susie asked.

The woman dropped her eyes to Susie. "Well, hello there. How are you today, little one?"

"Fine," Susie said curtly. "Are you here to play with us? I don't see you with any games."

The woman laughed, igniting a storm of wrinkles that consumed her face. "No, little one. I do not have any—"

"Is there something I can do for you?" Lucy cut in, stepping beside Susie and putting a protective hand on her shoulder.

The woman's eyes shot up, and the humor in her aged face instantly vanished. "Oh. Hello to you, ma'am. I'm sorry if I'm intruding on your time right now. I didn't know when would be a good time to stop by, to be honest."

"Are you from the church down the street?" Lucy asked. "I gave a donation to them just two weeks ago, so I'm afraid other charities are on my list at the moment."

"No, ma'am." She stared at Lucy in silence for a moment, making Lucy feel scared and uncomfortable. Right when Lucy was about to tell her goodbye, the woman spoke again. "Lucy Gold. It *is* you. My God... I never thought I'd really find you."

Lucy's hazel eyes widened, but soon narrowed in confusion. "I'm sorry, do we know each other? How do you know my name?"

"Do you mind if I come in for a second? It's a bit of a long story, but I promise not to take up too much of your time."

"I don't know about that," Lucy said, moving her hand from Susie to the door. "I generally don't—"

"Please... I've come a long way to find you. I assure you I'm not up to anything."

Lucy locked eyes with her, once again standing in silence.

Had it been any other person, Lucy would have decided that the situation was just too dangerous to risk the proposal. The bygone decades had sapped her strength to defend herself, and Susie was much too young to fend off an aggressor.

But this lady was just as old as she was, perhaps even more so. Besides, something in the woman's tired eyes told Lucy that she could trust her. That she was, in the lady's own words, not up to anything.

"Okay," Lucy agreed. "Just for a short bit though. This little girl here needs a nap pretty soon, and I might join her, so..."

"Oh thank you, Lucy. Yes, I completely understand. I'm off like the wind as soon as you need me to leave."

"What's off like the wind mean?" Susie asked her.

The woman giggled at Susie.

Lucy glanced at her granddaughter. "I'll explain later, sweetie."

CHAPTER 29

The old woman supplied her first name (Trisha) before she took a sip of iced tea, leaving a thin water ring on the glass patio table as she lifted the cup to her lips and took three large gulps.

"Pardon me," Trisha said with embarrassment, putting a hand to her mouth as she lowered the cup back down. "I've been very thirsty walking around with that hot sun on me. I really appreciate your generosity."

"It's nothing," Lucy said, sitting down across the table from her and briefly glancing at a butterfly dancing over her rosebushes in her backyard. Susie, legs dangling as she combed the tangled hair of a doll, was next to Lucy, lost in her playful tiny world. "Where are you traveling from, exactly?"

"Really far from here, I'm afraid. Many miles and motels."

"Canada?"

"No. Not that way. Your home state, Lucy. A few hours from where you grew up. It *was* Lake Sabrina, right? That's what I remember you saying in the film."

"That's correct." Lucy stiffened, crossing her arms. "Oh no. You're not here because of *South to North*, are you? Looking for an autograph or something?"

Trisha shook her head. "No. I'm many years past that sort of silliness. My eyes couldn't bear all those highway lines if it weren't for something very important. It's the only thing that kept me going while driving through all those states."

Lucy shooed a fly from her face. "I don't understand. Why are you here? Why are you looking for me?"

Trisha's eyes shifted to Susie, then back to Lucy. "You might want to have her take that nap now. I don't think a girl her age should hear what I have to say."

"Well, we're not going to be swearing like sailors, are we? She should be fine out here."

Trisha leaned over the table. In a voice barely loud enough to hear, she whispered, "This is about your mother, dear. Susan Gold."

Lucy's mouth parted in surprise. She immediately fixed her focus on Susie. "It's nap time now, sweetie. Head on to your bed."

Susie's brow stitched together. "Aww, but Grandma… You said I could play until she was like the wind."

"Off like the wind. I know, sweetheart. I'm sorry. But we have grown-up things to discuss. Go on, now. Don't let me catch you playing around, either. I will check on you."

Susie lowered her head, her beautiful blonde curls hiding her disappointed face. "Yes, Grandma. I'll go."

She slid the sliding glass back door open, closed it, and walked off.

Lucy peered through the glass until she could no longer see Susie.

"She's beautiful, Lucy. Like a perfect doll. You are a very blessed grandma."

"Thank you. That's kind of you to say. But I'm not sure I'll be thinking about how blessed I am today. Who are you? What do you know about my mother?"

Trisha took another sip of her iced tea, her hand trembling slightly. Lucy couldn't determine if it was because she was nervous, or because of her aged frailty.

"My last name is Cain. Trisha Cain. I was born in the small town of Bishop, a place you might know about because it's only a few hours north of Lake Sabrina. Just straight up on I-395. I barely have any memories of the place because I wasn't there long. When I was a few years younger than your granddaughter, my mother moved me to Eugene in Oregon, telling everyone at the time that she couldn't take the government drought restrictions any longer. That she needed to find a better life away from California."

"A lot of people went that direction," Lucy said. "I had a cousin whose family made that same move. She's still in Oregon to this day."

"Yes, but our reasons for leaving weren't as pure as my mother wanted people to believe. You see, she was having an affair with a man who was living with another woman. I didn't find out about it until I was seventeen, when I accidently came across a shoebox filled with notes and photographs of a strange person I'd never met. It was in my mother's dresser. I was only looking for a bra to borrow for a date I had that night; what I found was a secret that completely destroyed my relationship with my mother."

Trisha paused for a minute, watching the same fly that had darted around Lucy's face now scurry across the wrinkled, paper-thin skin of her own hand. She waited until it flew off before continuing.

"His name was Ted Burrows. She met him when visiting a friend in Lake Sabrina. Their encounter was actually at the end of her trip, when she stopped by an auto shop to replace an air filter for her car. Ted walked right up to her and told her exactly the right part she needed. My mother said he even helped her put it in her car. If you ask me, he was helping to put it in all right. Many times over in the course of the next six months."

Lucy's sharp mind was laser-focused on Trisha's words. Her mouth was open in a circle and her eyes seemed glued in place. "She was that taken by him?"

Trisha nodded, then shrugged. "My mother was very young and naïve. She had insecurity issues, too. It didn't take much to keep her on his leash, to get her to keep driving back to your town just to shack up in motels. Sometimes those flings would be at her house in Bishop, when he could break away from his woman."

"My mom," Lucy said, the words spilling out like a cough.

"Yes. My mother knew her name because Ted let it slip the first day they had sex, the idiot he was. Susan Gold. That name has haunted me my entire life, Lucy. I tell you the truth it has."

"The documentary..." Lucy said, thinking ahead. "The director asked me my name, then asked that I tell a little bit about my family. That's how you knew."

"I couldn't believe it when I heard what you said on film. I first thought my ears were deceiving me. It was impossible that I was listening to the daughter of the same Susan Gold my mother had told me about. The same Susan Gold my mother had—"

Trisha's voice cut off. She tried to take another sip of her drink, but both hands were now shaking wildly. She stuffed them between her legs, closed her eyes while drawing in a deep breath, and looked at Lucy.

She forced the word out. "Murdered."

The sound hung in the air like a brick waiting to crash through the glass table, spraying fragments like a fountain. The word drowned out all noises, all perception of the outside world, of reality. It erased not only the present, but the future and past in one sweep. Time seemed frozen for both women. It was as if their long lives were meant to intersect at that moment—two climbers meeting face-to-face at the summit of a mountain after years of independently ascending the same steep cliffs and rugged terrain.

A thousand years could have easily slipped by unseen in the abyss of that moment.

Lucy almost spoke first, but Trisha beat her to it. "I hate to ask this, but do you have a cigarette?"

"Sorry, I don't smoke," Lucy replied.

"That's smart. I haven't for ages either. But now, the urge is almost overpowering. It's like I never quit."

Vulnerable times, Lucy.

151

Uncle Neil's voice seemed to echo in Lucy's mind. She was glad she had never started and couldn't offer Trisha one at this susceptible moment.

Trisha bit down on her lip to fight the desire. "My mother loved Ted in a crazy way I'll never understand. She was teased and abused by him, and she even knew of the evil things he was doing to your mom, cheating included. She was blind to all of it. She went insane when things went south with Ted and Susan because he said he didn't want to see her anymore. She was several months pregnant with me when that happened. I know in my heart that's why he really stopped seeing her, his screw girl was now getting too fat and had luggage, but my mom swore it was because of Susan. She only became more convinced when they later found him dead and your mom was locked up."

"I'll never forget my grandma telling me she didn't believe the story behind my mother's death," Lucy said. "They claimed it was a stabbing in the cafeteria over contraband. Made it appear drug related."

"Your grandma was absolutely right. It was a lie. A huge one. My mother only told one person about the truth, and that was me. I think it was to get the guilt off her chest. Whatever the case, she told how she knew a coworker who knew a security guard at the prison. She secretly stole the contact information for the guard. She then bribed the guard who in turn bribed a prisoner who was already serving a life sentence. Nothing was ever traced back to my mother. The closest it ever came was when her coworker asked a few questions about the killing. That was when she decided to move to Oregon. She had to distance herself from it."

"The coworker never said anything more?"

Trisha shook her head. "No. And neither did I. In all this damn shitty time, neither did I. I let my mother get away with the monstrous crime she'd committed. I kept silent as a teenager. I kept her secret as a young adult. I kept it when I got married and had a baby of my own. I kept it when my mom got brain cancer and passed away. I kept it when my husband and I divorced. And I kept it when my baby told me Oregon wasn't far enough north that he was moving to Washington and leaving me behind."

Tears welled in Trisha's eyes, then started to flow in streams through the deep wrinkles on her face. Her bottom lip quivered as she stared at Lucy, barely able to speak.

"Then I come here, and I see your beautiful life. Your wonderful house. Your gorgeous granddaughter. Everything amazing you've created for yourself and others around you. And I think thank God, Lucy. Thank God my half sister moved on from the awful pain we put in her life. The damn evil we created. The agony we must have caused you. Thank God almighty you don't have people like us anymore stealing your rainbows. Trampling your flowers."

Trisha covered her face with her pale, spotted hands and cried.

Lucy immediately moved to her, hugging her with one arm over her shoulder.

"Trisha..." Lucy whispered her name slowly. "It was years and years ago. Besides, it was your mother, not you. You didn't do anything."

"I did, though. I did by not doing. I could have said something, Lucy. I could have made things better. I've had such guilt for it. Such God-awful guilt."

Lucy tightened her arm around her, and spoke softly. "My mom was already gone. You couldn't have brought her back. Nobody can change what happened to her. And as for your guilt, you did what you needed to do just by being brave and coming here. That's enough for me. There's no reason to carry it anymore."

Trisha nodded, but it was impossible to tell if she'd truly heed Lucy's words after carrying the shame for so long. All she could do at the moment was cry beside her stepsister as the sun inched its way west.

And there the two women sat as one in the still, silent afternoon. California was somewhere far beyond the horizon. Not as far was a room covered in flowers and rainbows—a wallpaper design that would have made Trisha believe that she had prescient powers had she known about the interior decoration. In that room slept a little girl, dressed in yellow, whose story had only just begun in Maine.

PART V
LUCY'S LETTER

CHAPTER 30

Lucy stared up at the marble and limestone masterpiece, marveling at the sculptor's attention to detail: the folds on the pants, the artful position of the hands on the side of the chair, the waves of the thinning hair, the stubby terrain of the beard. She felt a powerful sense of awe looking at the statue. It was as if she were standing at the foot of the living person, the man whom she had admired since days unremembered, a palpable sense of urgency—both in his era and hers—electrifying the air.

Lucy supposed the Lincoln Memorial had that effect on a lot of people.

It was barely seven in the morning, but crowds were already gathering on the memorial's steps and around the Reflecting Pool in anticipation of what was expected to be the largest march in human history. An estimated four million people were projected in Washington D.C. alone. The streets of London and Paris had already felt the shoes of a united three million. Vancouver was supposed to have a strong two and a half million showing, Seattle would have three million, and Beijing, scheduled the next day, was projected to be the largest at six million.

In truth, it was nearly impossible to accurately count the number of people participating in what was internationally labeled the *E1* march. It was easier to total the cities involved, three hundred and sixty four, than the shifting mass of humanity demanding stricter measures to save their endangered planet.

E1 stood for *Earth First.* What was at stake wasn't the rocky exterior and core of the planet itself—that had revolved around the sun for billions of years and would continue to circle it for billions more whether humans were around or not. Rather, the *E1* movement was for the life that was fading into extinction. It was a march to put a spotlight on the destruction that had already been done—the millions of species that had vanished, the swelling human death toll—as well as to show the necessity for all governments to put the environment as the top priority to prevent future devastation.

"Is that *the* Abraham Lincoln?"

Lucy glanced down at Mary, who wore a red dress and stood between Jimmy and Shannon. Her older sister was behind her, wearing sunglasses and a new blue shirt that read *We1 at E1*.

"Who else would it be, goofball?" Susie asked Mary, softly bopping the top of Mary's head with her hand. "It's not George Washington."

"Be nice, Susie," Shannon said, picking Mary up so she could have a better view from Shannon's arms. "It's pretty neat, huh?"

"He was a really big president!" Mary added. "Did he have other big chairs like that?"

Lucy and her family burst out laughing.

Mary looked at them, confused. "What?"

"I've got something for you, honey." Jimmy said, removing a backpack from his shoulders and unzipping it. "You too, Mom. I've got two things for you."

Jimmy took out a card with Shannon and Lucy's names written in cursive on the front envelope.

"Jimmy, you didn't need to get us anything today," Lucy said, taking it. "You already paid for this trip."

"I know, but the kids and I wanted to. Now it's all on recycled paper, so don't worry about that part. That would be some irony today if it weren't."

Lucy moved next to Shannon and opened it so they both could read the text.

Faith, Hope, Love

Thank you, Mom

You are the living embodiment of all that is eternal

Happy Mother's Day

Jimmy, Susie, Mary

"Aww, Jimmy..." Lucy said, looking to her son. She embraced him as if she were saying goodbye forever, moved by the card. "I love you."

"Thank you, honey," Shannon added, joining the embrace as best she could while holding Mary. "I love you, too."

"And you two thought they couldn't pull it off this day!" Jimmy said, turning to the growing crowd behind them. "What did you say again? Mother's Day has no room for a Mother Earth march?"

"You were right," Lucy said, smiling in the direction of the crowd. "I admit when I'm wrong. It's stunning to see." She turned to him. "You said you had something else for me. What is it?"

"Oh yeah!" Jimmy said, reaching in his backpack again. He removed a folded letter that was yellow with age. The handwritten words upon it pressed out the paper. He smiled coyly as he gave it over.

"What is this?" Lucy said, unfolding it. She saw it was in her own handwriting.

"I saw this two years ago when moving some boxes in your garage. I remember asking what you would write." He shook his head with wonder, smiling. "I never knew you took it seriously and wrote a letter out."

"Oh, this old thing?" Lucy laughed, skimming it silently.

"What is it, Grandma?" Mary asked.

"Yeah, Grandma," Susie said, leaning in. "What does it say?"

"Me first! Me first!" Shannon said jokingly.

Lucy shook her head, then gave Jimmy a scolding glance. "See what you created now?" Turning to the children, she said, "It's just foolishness. It was just me getting out my frustrations one day. I used to keep a journal when I was a kid, and I guess I wanted to play a little game of pretend in writing this. It was years ago."

"Guess you'll just have to read it to us. It seems proper. I saw you tied in a few words from Lincoln's Gettysburg address. It's why I brought it today. And if Lincoln had to read his speech, then…"

"Jimmy…" Lucy said shyly.

"Come on Grandma, please, please," Mary begged. "I want to hear!"

Lucy glanced at her family, wanting to say no, but shook her head in surrender and read the words that had come from the marrow of her soul. She heard her voice softly echo inside the Lincoln Memorial (a pitch higher than the commotion of the crowd) to the point where the words seemed like birds flying around the marble structure, threading the pillars. She spoke clearly, steadily, and beautifully. It was as if she'd been practicing for weeks to say it aloud.

When she finished, her children and grandchildren stared at her with a surreal fascination that she would never forget. They seemed to be gazing at a celebrity or some notable public speaker. She felt like a little girl again—insecure, wanting to run and hide.

First there was silence, then clapping.

A few others who had eavesdropped on the speech added to their applause.

"Thank you," Lucy said, blushing. "You are very kind. It's nothing big."

"It's wonderful, Mom." Jimmy said with pride. He showed her another letter, a white one, and took out a tape dispenser. "I've been planning for this day. I'm going to tape up a copy of what you wrote and leave it here for people to see."

"What? You really are digging yourself in a hole with me, Jimmy! You know that?"

"Well, I don't think you want my version of that letter up there. You remember what I wanted to say, what I told you?"

"I do, and we shall not repeat it around the children."

"Of course not. But *your* letter goes up. I want more people to read it. And I get to play pretend just like you did. Like we talked about that day."

"What do you mean?"

"I'm imagining this letter can go back in time. It will reach people who were born many generations before us, people who have a real chance to preserve the Earth the way they saw it back then. Before the damage became irreversible."

"Even in your little fantasy, sweetie, what makes you think they would care? And how would they spread the word even if they did?" Shannon asked, staring at him incredulously.

Jimmy turned to her. "They'd care because they've already seen some of the warning signs in their time, just like Mom mentioned in the letter. They'd see the road it leads down, what's happening to us now, and they'd want a better future for the Earth and their descendants. The family members who will carry their name and blood."

"Dad, that's crazy optimistic, don't you think?" Susie asked. "I agree with Mom that they'd never get enough people involved. They'd think the letter is too preachy or moralistic. It'd reach only a handful who wanted to do something, and then just die like a forgotten book."

"Not if the few who understood its importance used hashtags for the letter, or shared posts with their friends about it, or posted videos giving the same speech Grandma just did." Jimmy saw Susie flash him a bewildered look. He continued, "We aren't sending the letter back to the Stone Age, Susie. I'm talking about a time during the birth of social media. When they had the means to quickly share what was important. I did a little studying on the technology they had back then. That's how I found out about hashtags."

"But this all just fantasy, Dad! What's the point of any of it?"

"I believe in Daddy!" Mary joyously retorted to her sister. "I like pretend!" Mary reached out to her father.

Jimmy took her in his hands and said, "Ha! See! I've got one girl who wants to play! How about you, Grandma? Do you want to help tape it up?"

Lucy's head drew back in surprise. "What? You mean put that copy on a wall or something?"

"I was thinking one of the pillars. I like the symbolism of it."

"Jimmy, I'm pretty sure security is going to get mad at us. They'll think we are vandalizing."

He laughed. "With this crowd around us, Mom? You could probably sit in Lincoln's lap and no one would notice."

"I doubt that."

"Okay, yes, that's a bit extreme. But you get my point." Jimmy looked at his family, Mary mimicking his enthusiasm. It was hard to tell who was more excited—the four-year-old girl, or the forty-six-year-old father whose brilliant blue eyes flashed with the same childlike delight. He motioned his family toward the nearest pillar. "Come on, guys! All of us! We do it, and then go join the march."

Jimmy strode up to the massive pillar, which was as thick as a sequoia tree, and put Mary right where its rounded base disappeared into the slick marble floor.

"You get the special job of giving us our tape. You think you can handle that?"

"I've got it!" Mary tore off a small piece, handing it to her father.

"Shannon, you first."

He held the letter as flat as he could while she secured the top of it.

Mary gave him more tape.

"Susie and Lucy, you guys next."

Susie taped the bottom. Lucy, still nervous about the security, glanced around like a criminal stealing the Hope Diamond, then quickly put her tape on, barely connecting it to the paper and wall.

"Me next!" Mary said. "I can't reach it, though."

Jimmy lifted her up, holding her as carefully as he could while she taped the side.

"You're the last one, Dad," Susie said, no longer objecting to the plan. The tone of her voice revealed that she was actually enjoying the rebellious nature of it.

Jimmy took the final strand of tape, put it on the only side that hadn't been secured, and nodded in approval. On the bottom of the copy was the hashtag he had included from doing his research: #LucysLetter.

"Godspeed to us all," Jimmy said, giving it a quick salute. He grabbed Shannon and Susie's hands and led them down the memorial's steps.

Lucy glanced at the letter a final time, pondering the fantasy of it traveling back through the history of the global CO_2 measurements, gauged in parts per million: to 800ppm, to 600ppm, to 400ppm. She thought about Susie's point that readers might interpret the message as too preachy or moralistic, and she hoped with all her heart that the words she had written down did not stray from her intent—to foster peaceful action, not guilt or blame.

She closed her eyes and whispered a dedication for the moment—for her beloved, who had passed the same year of Mary's birth. "Wherever you are, Adam. I miss you, love."

She then took her granddaughter's tiny hand and followed her family toward the Lincoln Memorial Reflecting Pool, the morning sun on their shoulders. They did not look back, nor did they speak of the letter for the rest of the march, accepting the reality that time travel was a fairy tale, yet wishing that Earth, somehow, could still have its happy ending.

CHAPTER 31

A House on Fire Cannot Stand

To the Children of the New Millennium:

Many score years will pile as high as a mountain and stretch as wide as a great river in the eras following your generation. The decisions you make during your brief stay on this borrowed planet determine whether that mountain, in the lens of time, is capped with snow and embraced by the beauty of scented evergreens, and whether that river is pure with fresh rain and flowing in abundance for tomorrow's farms and communities. The statutes and policies you set regarding the health of our shared home are not confined to the age in which you live. Those laws are stones thrown into the lake of Earth's history. The ripples spread with each succeeding generation—widening, growing, influencing—and become precedence for the subsequently tossed stones of legislation.

A house divided against itself cannot stand, nor can a house on fire. You must not turn a blind eye to the warning signs of rising temperatures, melting glaciers, violent storms, diminishing reservoirs, and burning forests. You must look with courage at the emergency which threatens our communal abode, and dedicate an unwavering, immediate focus—united in principle and policy—to snuffing out the peril smoldering in our midst. The hour of action is upon your generation. A newborn flame is manageable, but a mature inferno fed by the winds of denial, delay and indecisiveness becomes unstoppable. The great test of humanity's fate shall unfold in your lifetime, and will determine whether the children of tomorrow will inherit the embers of a lost paradise once ample with diversity and beauty, or whether they will live in comfort and peace in a house, a world, saved and preserved.

With love for all,

Lucy Gold & The Children of Tomorrow

#LucysLetter

Acknowledgements

My deepest thanks to:

My cover designer, Ellie Augsburger, for her artistic talent and professional advice.

My editor, Carl Augsburger, for his outstanding editorial skills in correcting my errors while preserving the voice of the story. You are a gifted man.

My young son, Conner Lowry, without whom I could not have written this book. I love you.

My parents, Sandra and James Lowry, for their constant support and warmth.

The many scientists, journalists, and photographers who make the environment their life's work. You are unsung heroes.

And the readers who care about #LucysLetter. Thank you for spreading the word, and for putting our house, our planet, first.

Between every two pine trees there is a door leading to a new way of life.

-John Muir

www.ingramcontent.com/pod-product-compliance
Lightning Source LLC
Chambersburg PA
CBHW050943120626
46552CB00001B/355